WHATEVER DOESN'T KILL YOU

ELIZABETH WENNICK

ORCA BOOK PUBLISHERS

Library and Archives Canada Cataloguing in Publication

Wennick, Elizabeth, 1972-
Whatever doesn't kill you / Elizabeth Wennick.

Issued also in electronic formats.
ISBN 978-1-4598-0083-0

I. Title.
PS8595.E5593W43 2013   jc813'.54   C2012-907463-2

First published in the United States, 2013
Library of Congress Control Number: 2012952946

Summary: When the man who murdered Jenna's father is released from prison,
Jenna decides to confront him.

*Orca Book Publishers is dedicated to preserving the environment and has printed this book on
Forest Stewardship Council® certified paper.*

Orca Book Publishers gratefully acknowledges the support for its publishing
programs provided by the following agencies: the Government of Canada through
the Canada Book Fund and the Canada Council for the Arts, and the Province of British
Columbia through the BC Arts Council and the Book Publishing Tax Credit.

Cover image and design by Teresa Bubela
Author photo by Beth Downey Curry

ORCA BOOK PUBLISHERS
PO Box 5626, Stn. B
Victoria, BC Canada
V8R 6S4

ORCA BOOK PUBLISHERS
PO Box 468
CUSTER, WA USA
98240-0468

www.orcabook.com
Printed and bound in Canada.

16 15 14 13 • 4 3 2 1

To Jennifer Kovacic,
who only got to read the first part.

THURSDAY

I was six days old when Travis Bingham murdered my father. I've made my brother, Simon, tell me the story a thousand times: how Travis held up my dad's store, how my dad was already giving him the money, how Travis shot him anyway and left him to die on the floor in a pool of blood, the money scattered all over the floor and a ten-dollar bill still clutched in his hand.

I've seen the newspaper clippings too; Simon has them all in a file folder in a box in the basement that he doesn't know I've looked through every chance I've had. There are stories in there from the days and weeks right after it happened, articles about what a great guy my dad was, a real "pillar of the community." There are pictures of

1

him with the kids' softball team he sponsored, pictures of him grinning with Simon and my sister, Emily. They all say how tragic it was that his days-old baby (that's me) would never get to know him, and there are pictures of my mom standing in front of my dad's boarded-up store, holding little me and looking sad. Travis had turned eighteen a week before the botched robbery, old enough for an adult trial. His high school picture was plastered all over the papers, him shaggy-haired and surly and looking every bit like a killer should look. I've spent hours looking at that picture, enough time to memorize every contour of his face, every pimple, every fleck in those cold, yellow-green eyes.

And they're the same eyes, even in black and white, staring back at me now from yesterday's paper, which someone has left on our table at McDonald's. I don't know how long I've been staring into them, like I'm expecting him to blink, to turn tail and run, to do some-thing other than stare out of the picture on page A8, but finally Griffin pokes me and I snap back to reality.

"Jenna? Everything all right?"

Marie-Claire laughs. "That's the longest I've ever heard you go without talking," she says.

"You're funny." I look at the paper again and reluctantly fold it up. I turn my attention back to the group at our table:

WHATEVER DOESN'T KILL YOU

besides me, Griffin and Marie-Claire, there's my best friend, Katie Becker. We're camped out in the corner of McDonald's, as far away from the busy counter and the kids' PlayPlace as we can manage.

We come here once or twice a week for lunch, the four of us. There aren't a lot of kids from our school who make the trek here at lunch hour, and the throngs of stay-at-home moms who bring their kids here to let them tear around the indoor playground while they sit and chat are a nice change from the cafeteria crowds.

Griffin and Katie and I have known each other since grade three. Marie-Claire, who is a year older than us, was the loser at her school out on the east coast before we all met up in high school last year. Marie-Claire went to a French school out east, so she's a year behind in English, which is where we met her. Katie gets mocked for her weight, me for my clothes, Marie-Claire for her thick French accent and Griffin for...well, being Griffin. Together, we're the Loser Club, an assortment of sore thumbs at a school full of punks and jocks and wannabe rappers.

Of course, they all know the story about my dad. It's hard to keep secrets in a group this small, and anyone who's been to my apartment is bound to ask why I live with my older brother and sister instead of my parents.

ling of suddenly seeing Travis Bingham—
s older and a little weathered-looking but
absolutely, unmistakably him—where I expected to find
the comics page…well, I'm not ready to share that just yet.

Katie's the only one still eating—two double quarter-
pounders with cheese, a Coke and an extra-large order of
fries. Griffin has finished his Happy Meal with chicken
nuggets and is playing with the toy that came with it,
a little stuffed bear with a tiny pink T-shirt you can put
on and take off. He is drawing a skull and crossbones on
the front of the shirt with a Sharpie. I'm surreptitiously
picking at the contents of the bag lunch I brought from
home and tucked into the corner beside me so the staff
won't see me eating my own food and throw us out. I'm
broke this week: none of my babysitting clients have paid
me in awhile, so even a couple of bucks for a hamburger
is out of the question.

I force some small talk. "I can't believe how cold it's
been all week."

"I hear it's supposed to warm up next week. We're
supposed to get snow on Wednesday."

Katie shakes her head between bites of hamburger.
"You can't trust the long-range forecast. It's got, like,
a thirty percent chance of being right."

"I could probably have a thirty percent success rate if I just made something up." Griffin chortles. He always laughs before he says something he thinks is going to be funny. "I predict three weeks of sunshine and thirty-degree temperatures, followed by hurricanes, and crickets falling from the sky."

Griffin is such a geek that he says thank you if you call him one. He also answers to "nerd," but he draws the line at "dork." He reserves that word for the few kids lower on the social totem pole at school than he is. You'd think someone who's had his ass kicked twice a week since kindergarten would want to spare other people the same treatment, but frankly, he can be a bit of a jerk sometimes.

When I think no one's looking, I carefully roll up the entire section of the newspaper with Travis's picture in it and tuck it into my tie-dyed messenger bag alongside my school books, hoping no one has noticed me taking it. I don't think we'd really get kicked out of McDonald's for stealing an old newspaper, but since I didn't buy anything in the first place, I'd hate to push my luck.

Griffin catches up to me as we wait for the lights to change at the Delta, where Main Street switches from one-way to two-way—or vice versa, I suppose, depending on which way you're going. Ordinarily I don't pay a lot of attention to traffic lights, especially when it's this cold out. If there are no cars coming, I'll take my chances and run across. But crossing the Delta means making an odd hop, skip and jump across three separate intersections, and jaywalking here means taking your life in your hands. Even crossing with the lights is sometimes more dangerous than a trip to McDonald's is worth.

"So what's with the newspaper?"

I should have figured he'd be the one to notice. Not much gets past Griffin Paul. "Nothing," I tell him, determined to be mysterious. "Just an interesting story."

Griffin doesn't buy it. "Marie-Claire's right: you're never quiet. Come on, what was so interesting that you'd take the newspaper?"

"It wasn't anything big. It really wasn't." I struggle for a lie, but nothing comes to mind. "There was a story about some software company making a donation to this halfway house so criminals can learn to type and get jobs after they're released back into the community." Which is technically true: that is what the article was about.

"Well, that definitely sounds like an article worth holding on to."

I try to think of some reason I might have wanted to keep the article—a school project it might relate to, a personal interest it might have piqued. But I can't come up with anything. So I tell him the truth. "Travis Bingham is out of jail."

From across the street in the middle of afternoon traffic, Marie-Claire hears what I say to Griffin and jogs across at the light to catch up with us.

Now, I should tell you, Marie-Claire thinks she's a vampire. For real. She wears black clothes and silver chains and goes to parties with university kids who think she's nineteen. They drink vodka and tomato juice and pretend it's blood. Of course the other kids at school mock her relentlessly, but that's why she hangs out with us. If she didn't have a place with the rest of the losers, she wouldn't have any age-appropriate friends at all. But I swear, sometimes I wonder if there might be something to this whole vampire thing. It's like she's got superhuman hearing sometimes.

"No kidding," she says. "The guy who killed your dad is out of jail?"

"I guess so, if he's in a halfway house."

"I thought he got twenty-five years."

"That doesn't mean anything." Katie has caught up to us too; she's pushing three hundred pounds and doesn't have a lot of "hustle." Despite lagging a few steps behind the rest of us, though, she seems to have caught up on the gist of the conversation. "If you don't get in any trouble in prison, you automatically get out after you serve two-thirds of your sentence. Plus, if you're in jail for, say, two years while you're waiting for your trial, you get credit for four years."

Katie can be a know-it-all, but it's hard to argue with her when she really does seem to know it all sometimes.

Marie-Claire grabs my arm, her black-painted fingernails digging into the ratty fabric of my coat so hard I can feel them through my clothes.

"We have to go see him," she says.

"What?" It takes me a second to even process what she's said.

"Travis What's-his-face. Burnham."

"Bingham."

"Whatever. Don't you want to confront him?"

"Well, I…" I frown. "I guess I've never really given it much thought."

I don't think I've ever seen Marie-Claire smile before, but she's grinning now with an almost hungry look in her washed-out green eyes. "Come on, you've known about this guy your whole life. He ruined your entire family, and now here he is, out in the world where you could just walk right up and talk to him? Where is this place? We have to go!"

"I don't even know what I would say to him," I protest.

"You'll know," she says, her voice dripping with melo-drama. "You'll see him and you'll know exactly what you're supposed to say. We'll go with you. We can go after school."

"I can't tonight. I've got to meet the kids at the bus."

"Well, then, tomorrow."

"I can't go tomorrow. I've got to work after school," Katie chimes in. Apparently this is a group activity now.

"Saturday then," says Griffin. He pushes his heavy glasses up his long, pointy nose. "You don't have to babysit this Saturday, do you?"

"I'll…have to check my schedule," I manage. But I'm a lousy liar. Without any particular input from me, it's been decided. We—the four of us—are going to stalk Travis Bingham.

* * *

After school I'm late meeting the kids' bus, and I have to stand on the corner behind a herd of women from my apartment building, all of them smoking, chatting on their cell phones and ignoring their screaming kids in strollers. I don't know why they always have their phones pressed up to their ears when there is a perfectly serviceable group of people they could talk to standing right beside them.

It's not like they're discussing anything earth-shattering; mostly who is newly pregnant, who is newly split-up, who is cheating on whom with whom. If they would all just share this news with the people standing at the bus stop every day, I'm sure they would all have much lower cell-phone bills. Once or twice I've heard them complaining about how unfair it is that the superintendent is after them for not paying their rent on time, but since the superintendent is my brother, Simon, they've started looking over their shoulders a little more frequently to make sure I'm not standing there.

I'm picking up five kids today. Some days it's seven or eight, and some days it's just two or three. But today I have Carlie and Courtney, the twins from 304, who are seven; Henry from 521, who is five; Xavier from 107, who is ten and really too old to need a babysitter; and Wex, of course. Wex is my nephew—my sister Emily's son—and he lives with us. So does Emily, allegedly, although I haven't seen her in a couple of days.

On nicer days we go to the park for an hour, and the kids' parents are usually home by the time we get back, but on miserable, cold days like this one, we just hang out in my apartment for the hour or so. It's like Jenna's After-School Fun Club, only it's not really all that much fun.

Mostly they spend the hour fighting over who gets to play with Wex's PlayStation.

Still, there are worse things I could do to make a buck, and it's the twentieth of the month so I know everyone's Baby Bonus will be in the bank today. Odds are, I'll at least have enough money to buy lunch tomorrow.

Outside, the air smells like a giant fart, from the sulfur and crud the side-by-side steel plants down the street are spewing into the air. Inside the apartment building, the hallway smells like fish and old socks. Henry holds my hand all the way down the hall to our apartment, which would be cuter if he hadn't been wiping his runny nose on the back of his hand all afternoon. He always seems to have a cold, and his sleeve and hand are constantly covered in dried snot. Henry chatters away, telling me elaborate tales of his day, every couple of words followed by a question mark to make sure I'm still listening: "And then? We went? To the gym?"

The other kids chatter among themselves, except for Wex, whose hands are buried in the pockets of his scruffy gray coat; his chin is down against his chest. Poor kid: he's a ridiculous-looking little guy, with one huge front tooth that sticks almost straight out of his mouth and stringy hair that looks greasy about five minutes after it's washed. He's weird, too; talks to himself, lisps, trips on his own feet. The kids in our building aren't horrible to him. They just don't have a lot to say to him. I'm pretty sure he gets his ass handed to him at school though. Nobody that odd has a great time in elementary school. I should know.

The door is locked when we get home, but Simon's inside, stirring up some sort of pasta and canned soup in a casserole dish. I bang on the door till he lets us in, the dish still in his hands.

"Ooh, you're so do-*mes*-tic," I singsong. "What's for supper, jerk?"

"Worms and slug slime, you turkey," he singsongs back at me as the kids pour into the apartment. "Take your wet shoes off in the living room, you little punks."

"What'd you lock the door for?" I ask him.

"I didn't. Emily's home. She must have locked it."

Wex lights up, as much as he ever does. When he smiles, his lips peel back, showing off that massive snaggle-tooth of his. I think he's actually trying to train himself to keep his mouth closed as much as possible. He wasn't that cute a kid even before his adult teeth started coming in pointed every which way; now, he's just crazy-looking.

"Mom's here?" And he bolts off to the back bedroom that I sort of share with my big sister, his wonderful mother who hasn't seen her son since Saturday morning.

I follow him down the hall to throw my bag in the bedroom. Emily is sprawled out on the double mattress of the bottom bunk, snoring away. At least she's on it alone, for a change—I've found a number of different short-term houseguests there over the past couple of years, guys she's picked up at bars or parties and brought home for a "visit."

"Hey." I pick up a shoe from amid the clutter on the floor and toss it at her. "Rough night?"

Wex scowls. "Don't throw stuff at my mom," he says.

"Wex, Mommy's sleepy," she mumbles.

"That's okay." Wex slips into the bed with her and curls up beside her. "I'm pretty sleepy too."

I head back out to the living room, where the usual afternoon chaos is going on. Xavier's mother picks him up first, and gives me ten of the thirty dollars she owes me.

"My check was a little short," she says, not quite looking me in the eye. There's a brown paper bag tucked under one arm, so I'm sure the check wasn't quite as short before she stopped at the liquor store on her way home, but ten bucks is better than nothing, I guess.

"That's fine. You can get me the rest next week."

The twins' mother is next, and she gives me the full twenty she owes me. She's not a bad sort, even if she does smoke like a chimney and dress her kids alike, which is totally lame. At least she pays me on time and always says thank you when she picks them up. People don't say thank you nearly enough, if you ask me. Especially around here.

Henry's mother, Yolanda, still hasn't shown up by suppertime, so Simon sits him down at the kitchen table with a plate of the soupy casserole while I go call Wex for supper.

Henry is on his second plate of food by the time Wex starts picking at his first. I don't think Henry gets a lot to eat at home. Henry's mother is what Simon calls a "special case." There are a lot of those living in this building. Yolanda's got about four teeth left in her head, and you can barely understand a word she says, but somehow she's got a job at Nora's, a cruddy little coffee shop crammed into the corner of a strip mall, between a used-computer store and a payday-loan center. I've never been inside Nora's, so I have no idea how it stays in business. You can tell just by looking in the window that it's disgusting. Besides, this is Hamilton. There's a Tim Hortons on every corner. Why would anyone go to some roach-infested little hole-in-the-wall with crackheads behind the counter when they can go to good old reliable Timmy's? It seems un-Canadian to even think of it. But somehow the place stays in business, and somehow Henry's mom manages to show up to work there on what seems to be a fairly regular basis—or at least often enough not to get fired.

"So did your mom wake up and tell you where she's been for four days?" I ask Wex. He hunches over his supper and shrugs.

"She didn't wake up yet," he mumbles.

Henry chatters away, more stories that go nowhere. Nobody's listening, but he doesn't care.

"And my teacher? Mrs. Biggs? She said we could play? Outside on the playground?"

There's a knock on the door then, and Henry hops down off his chair and bolts to the door to see if it's his mom. Funny how Wex and Henry both have such crappy moms but are always so excited to see them.

Yolanda is more lucid than usual and has a big smile for Simon.

"Hey, cutie," she says. "Haven't seen you in awhile."

Simon smiles back, sort of. It's more of a grimace, really.

"You saw me yesterday. Right here. Right about this time."

"Was that just yesterday?"

"Yep. Sure was."

She giggles weirdly. "Whoops. I must have forgot."

"How about that."

Henry steps into his enormous yellow rubber boots and tromps off down the hall toward the elevator. Yolanda lingers, trying to flirt with my brother, who either has no clue what she's doing or is choosing to ignore it. Since Simon hasn't been on a date in…well, as long as I can remember, anyway…I figure it could go either way.

"Hey, Yolanda." I step out of the kitchen, where we're eating. "You got money for me yet?"

"Oh, sure, honey. How much I owe you?"

"Fifty bucks," I tell her, my voice flat.

"Okay." She fumbles through her big black purse, dropping loose cigarettes and wadded-up Kleenex on the floor of our entryway. Coins and wrapped candies fly everywhere before she pulls out a rumpled red bill and hands it to me. "There ya go, hun. Am I all caught up now?"

"Yeah. We're good."

Fifty dollars. I tuck it in my pocket, trying to look nonchalant but secretly feeling this weird little rush of excitement, like I'm suddenly rich. Usually if Yolanda gives me five bucks I'm impressed. Fifty has got to be some kind of minor miracle. With the money the other kids' moms gave me earlier, I'm feeling a little giddy with wealth. Now all I have to do is keep it away from my sister.

*   *   *

After supper Katie texts me: want to come over? My mom's going out. We can watch a DVD.

WHATEVER DOESN'T KILL YOU

Every text I've ever gotten from Katie is perfectly spelled and punctuated. I don't think she's ever made a spelling error. She's certainly never made a math error. She's been on the honor roll every year since I've known her. In fact, if it weren't for the size and shape of her, I'd say Katie Quinn was just about perfect. Fortunately, she doesn't really rub it in. Much.

By the time I've changed my clothes—fresh jeans with holes worn in the knees and almost all the way through the butt, but still decent enough to cover everything, and a long-sleeved T-shirt with a faded peace sign on the front—Emily is up and shuffling around the room.

"So where have you been all week?" Emily seems to have a headache, so I talk as loud as I can without actually shouting.

"My boyfriend's place."

"Boyfriend, huh? Did you get his last name this time?"

"Screw you."

"Screw you? That's an unusual name. Is it Russian?"

I have to duck to avoid the shoe she hurls at me. I make a quick stop at the bathroom mirror to check my hair, make sure it's still more or less restrained in the braid I forced it into this morning. My hair—crazy and orange and completely undisciplined—is as ridiculous as Wex's front tooth. I try to force it into submission with braids and hair elastics and bandanas, but it still manages to escape and do whatever it wants.

Wex is playing hockey on the PlayStation when I get out to the living room. I step into my worn-out sneakers without untying them.

"Where are you going?" Simon calls from his bedroom.

"Katie's."

"It's a school night."

"That's fine. Maybe some of her smarts will rub off on me and I'll do better in school tomorrow."

"Smart-ass."

"Twit."

"Turkey," he yells through the closed door.

* * *

Katie and her mother live in a crooked little white house on Cannon Street, two doors down from a variety store with food on the shelves that looks like it all expired sometime last century and right next to a house with a sheriff's notice taped to the door proclaiming that the property has been seized by the bank. Apparently, with all the partying and drug dealing going on among the previous inhabitants, nobody had bothered to pay the mortgage in awhile. The neighborhood has improved a little since then, but not by much.

Katie's mom opens the door before I knock, greeting me like a long-lost daughter.

"She's upstairs, honey. Did you eat dinner? There's meat loaf and pie."

"No thanks, Ms. Quinn. It smells amazing, but I already ate. I'll just go up and see Katie, if that's okay."

Katie's house is my favorite place to go. Katie has her own room, her mom leaves us alone except to offer us food, and, despite the neighborhood, the place always smells good, like Pine-Sol and cookies. Katie is sprawled on the beanbag chair in her room watching *Jeopardy!*

"Ah. tv for smart people."

Katie shrugs. "A lot of it's just pop-culture stuff. Some of it's common sense."

We watch the rest of the show with Katie shouting out every answer before the contestants do. One guy can't figure out how his buzzer works, and another one has minus two thousand dollars by the time Final Jeopardy rolls around; he has to leave the game before supplying the final question.

"That'd be me on that show. A big fat zero."

"Quit putting yourself down," Katie says. "You're plenty smart."

"Yep. Straight Cs. I'm some kinda genius."

"You just don't apply yourself, that's all. If you studied instead of coming over here to watch TV all the time, you'd be a straight-A student."

"Yeah, that's what it is. My bleak future is all your fault."

Katie hauls herself up out of the beanbag chair and pulls out a couple of DVD boxed sets from the bookshelf.

"So, what will it be tonight? *Cosby Show*? Or *Family Ties*?"

Ah, that's more like it. Katie knows what I like. I'm sure she'd rather be watching some chick flick on W or a documentary on the Discovery Channel, but she always indulges me with these cheesy old sitcoms. I mull it over. Which happy eighties family do I want to watch bicker over some inconsequential little problem, only to work everything out in twenty-two minutes flat? That's how long it takes to watch a half-hour TV show, once you take out all the commercials. I point to Bill Cosby in an awful sweater on the box in Katie's left hand.

"That one."

And so it goes. I lounge on Katie's bed while she flops back into the beanbag and we watch an entire disc of episodes. We don't say much, just laugh at the tacky clothes, the lame jokes, the silly dialogue. At the end of every episode, there are hugs and smiles and laughs, and everyone's happy again. Nobody has any real worries—not like Katie does, and not like I do. Theo Huxtable doesn't have to worry about getting his head shoved in the toilet, or anyone yelling "Boom, boom, fatty!" when he walks down the hall. Clair never has to warn her kids to stay away from Main Street and Kenilworth Avenue after dark, where the drunks and meth heads are roaming, and Rudy doesn't have to worry about what she's going to say to the man who killed her dad.

Katie and I don't talk about that though. It's right there, hanging over our heads the whole time, and I'm pretty sure that both of us want to talk about it, figure out what I should say when I meet him. My heart beats a little faster just thinking about it. But neither of us says anything. We just laugh along with the live studio audience, episode after episode, until we get to the end of the disc.

* * *

I take a bus home from Katie's, still thinking about Travis Bingham. What if he'd never come along? My dad wasn't rich like the fathers in all those old sitcoms, but it would be pretty cool to come home to a normal family instead of a weird brother and a messed-up sister with an odd little boy.

I unlock the apartment door, daydreaming about walking into an immaculately decorated house with lush curtains and an overstuffed couch instead of an old futon and sheets tacked up over the windows, to a mom and dad asking how my day went instead of the random collection of freaks that passes for my family.

Everyone's asleep, but Simon has left the living room light on for me so I don't trip over anything. I stop to turn it off, and the photo over the TV catches my eye. It's a picture of everyone in my family but me—I hadn't come along yet. They're all dressed in their Sunday best and smiling at the camera. There's Simon, who was fifteen or so at the time, and Emily, smiling with two front teeth missing, which would make her seven or eight, I guess, and my mom, skinny and pretty, and my dad, handsome and dignified and friendly-looking. But no me. I didn't come along until two years later, the afterthought baby. I never got to be in a family photo.

I stand with my hand on the lamp switch for a long time before I turn it off, staring at the picture and wondering about all the what-ifs: if Dad was alive; if Mom wasn't sick; if Simon hadn't had to spend his whole adult life taking care of everybody else; if Emily wasn't…well, Emily. If I had a normal life; that would really be something. Maybe Marie-Claire is right. Maybe I do need to track down Travis Bingham. He should know what he's cost me.

FRIDAY

"Hey, Jenna, didn't anybody tell you? They already gave peace a chance, freak."

Ned Street is a real witty guy. He's almost as hilarious as he thinks he is. Last week he stuck a picture of a hippo on Katie's locker. I took it off and threw it away before she saw it, but he's always got something else in store. Wedgies, name-calling, *kick me* signs—he does love the classics. Making fun of my sweater with the peace sign on it is nothing new. He makes stupid hippie cracks every time I wear it. He's pretty much got a nasty comment for every item of clothing I own, but the hippie jokes seem to be his favorite. His little posse is right there too;

WHATEVER DOESN'T KILL YOU

Ashley Walsh and Sam Fletcher, grinning away at Ned like he's some kind of celebrity.

"Thanks for letting me know, Ned. I'll be sure to bring that up at the next meeting." I slide my books into my locker and close the door before he can make fun of the pictures I've got posted inside: photos from old magazines I found in an antique store on Ottawa Street. Smiling hippies at Woodstock, the cast of *Growing Pains* grinning at the camera, happy flappers doing the Charleston.

Ned looks a little perplexed.

"What meeting?"

"The International Society of Creeps, Freaks and Weirdos. We meet on alternate Tuesdays. You're a little late to get on the agenda for this week's meeting, but I'll be sure to let them know at the next one."

This leaves him speechless for about ten seconds. Then he pulls a penny out of the pocket of his jeans, which are the kind where the rear end hangs down to the knees. He flips it at me.

"Here you go, Jenna. Why don't you go buy yourself a new pair of pants? Looks like those ones are all worn out."

Ashley makes a face as she turns away from me. "You can *totally* see her underwear through those pants," I hear her say.

* * *

In the cafeteria, Katie nibbles on salad and sips Diet Coke while Griffin and I have the Friday fish-and-chips special. Katie can put away enough food for four people most of the time, but she doesn't like to overindulge at school. She attracts enough attention from the resident jerks as it is.

"It dates back to ancient times," she tells us. "Fish on Fridays, that is. They would slaughter the meat on the first day of the week, which was Sunday, and by Friday it would be rancid, so they'd eat fish instead, because it was caught fresh every day."

Griffin scrunches up his nose and pushes a strand of long, stringy hair out of his eyes. "I don't think this was caught fresh any time in recent history. I think it actually might have been grown in a laboratory, as a matter of fact."

Marie-Claire picks apart a Rice Krispies square with her long black fingernails and shoves it, almost grain by grain, into her mouth.

"So, Jenna, what time are we going tomorrow?" she asks between bites.

"Oh. That. I hadn't really thought about it. I don't even really know where this place is." Nonsense, of course.

I've only checked it out on Google Street View about sixty times since I found the article yesterday. It's a big white house that looks like it's made of Lego blocks, tucked away on a downtown street amid sprawling hundred-year-old brick houses that have all been subdivided into three or four apartments each, the lawns paved into driveways and a cluster of mailboxes on each porch.

"I think we should go first thing in the morning," Katie says. "Like, seven thirty. Surprise him on his way out for the day, if he's allowed out on work release or something."

"What are we doing to do, knock on the door?" Griffin says around a mouthful of fish and chips.

Marie-Claire shakes her head. "No, no. We just wait across the street. Hang out on the corner and smoke and try to blend in."

"You're the only one who smokes—which is disgusting, by the way, and is going to kill you," I say. "And what if he doesn't come out all morning? Simon had the news on this morning, and it's supposed to be minus twenty with the windchill factor all weekend. I'm not standing around on a street corner for four hours in freezing weather." Plus, I fail to add out loud, every time I so much as think about talking to Travis Bingham, my stomach does somersaults.

"So what do you want to say?" Griffin asks.

I shrug. "I don't really know. I haven't really thought about it."

"I think you should just walk right up and kick him, right in the nuts," Marie-Claire says.

"Yeah, and get charged with assault," Katie chimes in with a disapproving scowl at Marie-Claire. "I think you should just start by telling him who you are and see what he says."

"And I think we should play cards," says Griffin. He pulls a deck of cards out of his book bag and starts to deal out a game of Asshole, our standard lunchtime diversion, and the conversation instantly switches gears, much to my relief.

"Who was the president last time?"

"Not me. I've been the asshole for about ten games now."

"Griffin's been an asshole for going on sixteen years."

"You're hilarious."

Asshole has to be the lamest card game going, but once you get into it, it's a lot of fun. The first person to lay down all their cards gets to be the president for the next round; the last person is the asshole and has to give their best cards to the president next hand. As we start laying down our cards, I relax a little. Tomorrow will bring whatever it brings. For now, I'm winning this game, and that's enough to take my mind off everything else.

SATURDAY

"Jenna! Your boyfriend is here!"

Wex is watching *Veggie Tales* on TV, sitting cross-legged on the couch. He's eating a bowl of store-brand Fruity-O cereal in his too-small Spider-Man pajamas with the cuffs coming off.

I let Griffin into the apartment. He's hopping back and forth from foot to foot to warm up, waving his glasses in the air to defog them, and his cheeks are bright red from the cold.

I give Wex a cuff across the ear on my way past. "He's not my boyfriend."

He throws a cushion at me. "He's a boy and he's your friend, so he's your boyfriend."

"How did you even get in the building?" I ask Griffin. "I didn't hear you buzz."

"Somebody's moving in. They've got the door propped open."

"Right. I forgot that was today. They're moving into 403."

"Was that where the potheads with all the cats lived?"

"No, that was 421; 403 was the old guy who almost burned down the building last year. He put a pot of water on to boil and fell asleep on the couch. Simon had to get all the ceilings redone, and the floors in 503 too."

Wex throws another cushion, knocking Griffin's glasses out of his hand. "You're drowning out the TV. Go someplace else and talk."

"That's fine. We're leaving anyway." Griffin puts his glasses back on and uses the offending cushion to smack Wex in the head, but not hard enough to hurt. Wex giggles and smacks him back, spilling the milk from his cereal on the couch in the process, but nobody says anything about it. Wex doesn't get in trouble much, and when he does something wrong it's usually so minor it's hardly worth calling attention to it. Besides, it was mostly Griffin's fault.

I've been on the fence all night about whether to even go out today. I got maybe an hour of sleep between tossing and turning, worrying about what I might say if I see Travis Bingham, and listening to Emily pounding away at the keyboard on the practically antique computer in our bedroom, chatting with some guy online until she finally went out to meet him at some after-hours club at three in the morning. I know all this because she left the chat window open and I skimmed through the highlights of the conversation before I switched over to chat with Katie, who was also wide awake at that time. I made a mental note of the guy's profile name—Skinny D—just in case Emily doesn't come back in a day or two. At least that way we'll have something to give the police when they go looking for her.

Katie was the one who finally convinced me we should at least drive by the place. "You don't have to talk to him or anything," she told me. "Just see if you can get a glimpse of him. Who knows? Maybe something brilliant will pop into your head and you'll wind up confronting him after all. Or maybe it'll be enough just to get a look at him."

And so Griffin and I venture out into the ridiculous cold—so cold the snot freezes in our noses the second we step outside—to hike the five blocks to Marie-Claire's to haul her out of bed.

I don't care if I look ridiculous: I'm bundled in an old coat of Simon's that makes me look like the Michelin Man, a fluffy hat and mittens I knit myself out of a bunch of mismatched yarn, and a pair of long johns under my track pants that make me waddle like a penguin. But at least I'm a warm penguin. Besides, it's Saturday, my day off from Ned Street and Ashley Walsh and all their clever little buddies. Nobody is going to mock me but Griffin, and I can always make fun of him right back.

Griffin, for his part, grouses the entire way: his hands are cold, his ears are cold. He's wearing a hoodie under his thin leather jacket, but the two layers combined aren't nearly enough to block the vicious wind, and I'm sure digging his hands into the pockets of his pants is making it tough to walk. Every piece of his clothing is designer-made and bought at some pricey boutique, but on his long, lanky frame somehow everything he wears hangs strangely and just looks odd. Griffin is as long and scrawny as Katie is short and round, and with his huge glasses and receding chin, he looks like some bizarre new species of exotic bird. The Long-Nosed Geek.

"Why don't you at least pull up the hood on your sweatshirt? That would give you one less thing to complain about anyway," I suggest.

"I don't want to mess up my hair."

"Good plan. I'm sure all the cheerleaders and fashionistas will be shocked to see you looking anything less than perfect."

* * *

Marie-Claire lives in a picture-perfect five-bedroom house with her parents, little sister and grandmother. In the summer her *mémère* spends just about every daylight hour outside in the yard. There are rosebushes and every color of flower you can imagine, and I'm pretty sure I've heard her singing in French to the plants. I've seen her crawling around the yard for hours at a time, and I swear she straightens the blades of grass one by one.

Marie-Claire's mother opens the door for us with a big smile. "Griffin, you must be so cold! Would you like something hot to drink?"

"No, thank you, Mrs. Boulanger. Is Marie-Claire ready?"

"*Mon dieu,* no." She gives a little laugh. "She is still sleeping. Maybe Jenna can go and wake her up?"

I've woken my sister after a two-day bender, but getting Marie-Claire out of bed is still a challenge. I plod up the stairs in my stocking feet and turn on the light in Marie-Claire's room, which doesn't make a huge amount of difference since the walls are painted black.

"Hey. Time to get up." I jostle her feet, pull back the blankets a little. Marie-Claire grunts and rolls over. "Come on. It's freezing out and you're the only one with a driver's license."

Finally she drags herself out of bed, wearing a red-and-white-striped T-shirt and a pair of pink pajama pants with teddy bears all over them. She catches me checking them out and shoots me a look that sends me scampering back downstairs to wait in the kitchen while she gets ready to go.

When Marie-Claire finally makes her appearance in the kitchen, she looks much more like herself. No more teddy-bear jammies; she's back to a half-inch layer of eyeliner and a dog collar and her thigh-high boots with the three-inch soles. I suspect she'll be colder than Griffin, but at least she has a car. Or, more accurately, her mother's baby-blue minivan. It's not exactly goth chic, but when you're almost seventeen with a brand-new driver's license, you don't want to get too picky about what you drive.

"So where are you going?" Marie-Claire's mother asks as we all wriggle back into our coats. I have more wriggling to do than everyone else, so I leave it to someone else to make up a story.

"We're going up to Limeridge Mall. Jenna needs a new winter coat." The lie comes seamlessly out of Marie-Claire's mouth, much like a dozen others she tells her mother in the course of a week. I suppose Simon's old coat looks bad enough that it's a perfectly plausible lie, because Marie-Claire's mother nods and gives me a pat on the shoulder. "They should be on sale now. As soon as the cold weather arrives, they suddenly bring out all the spring and summer clothes. I think you will find something nice for a good price."

I hadn't thought of getting a new coat up until this point, but apparently this battered old thing of Simon's makes me look like some kind of welfare case. Maybe something a little newer wouldn't be a bad idea. But not today.

Marie-Claire rubs her temples as we trudge down the driveway to the van. "Ugh. I am so hungover."

"What did you do last night?" As if I couldn't guess.

"I went to a party at the university. I made out with this guy. I couldn't even tell you his name if you paid me. It was so much fun. I'm telling you, Jenna, you have to come with me sometime."

"I don't think Jenna's a vampire party kind of girl. Shotgun." Griffin races to the passenger door of the van before I can get there and waits for Marie-Claire to unlock it. I climb in the back, which is fine by me anyway. I'd rather not be in the front seat if we see Travis Bingham. I don't think he'd recognize me from my baby pictures in the newspaper way back when, but there's something that feels...off...about this whole adventure, and it makes me glad to have the tinted back windows of the van to hide behind. Like we're doing something a little bit creepy. *Stalking.* That's more than a little creepy, I suppose.

Katie is waiting outside her house when we get there, shivering on the porch. I slide over and let her get into the seat beside me, and we're off.

The halfway house is tucked away on a long, quiet street a few blocks from downtown. There are strollers and wagons stacked on most of the porches, and a bicycle chained to the streetlight across the road. I wonder if the inhabitants of all these other houses know they're living steps away from a murderer.

"So what are you going to do if he comes out?" Katie asks me.

"I don't know."

"I think you should just walk up and spit on him." That sounds almost classy when Marie-Claire says it: *Speet on 'im.* But it's still a gross idea. Besides, on a day this cold, the spit would probably freeze in midair. And

ELIZABETH WENNICK

I don't even know if I'm going to get out of the van if he comes out.

"You should have written him a note," Katie says. "That way if he doesn't come out you could just go up and slip it in the mailbox."

"Saying what?"

"I don't know, like a victim impact statement or something. Tell him about how messed up your sister is, and how much you've missed out on because you had to grow up without a dad, and what happened to your mom, and—"

"All right. Let me out."

"What?"

"I'm getting out." I scramble to climb over Katie to get to the sliding door on the other side of her. "You guys go up to Limeridge or something. I've got my phone. We can meet up for lunch or something later."

Katie looks baffled. "But we wanted to be here for you."

"Yeah, I know. You guys are awesome. Really. But... this is kind of my thing, you know? I think I really need to do this on my own."

Marie-Claire looks crestfallen, like she's missing out on Christmas all of a sudden. Maybe it's something to do with her inner vampire, but she seems to get a kick

38

out of other people's unhappiness. I think she wanted to see a real blowout between me and Travis Bingham.

"Are you sure?" she says. "Because I don't mind waiting. We can just drive around the block a little until—"

"No, go. I'm sure of it. I'll just catch the bus up the Mountain and meet you later on."

I dig my hands into the pockets of Simon's old coat and watch the van turn the corner and disappear. I stare at the building across the street, just an ordinary building on an ordinary street. *This is insane*, I tell myself. *Are you just going to stand out here all morning? What if he's not even there? What if he's been released, or he's broken his parole and robbed another store and he's back in prison for another fifteen years? What if—*

I watch as the front door opens and a man steps out. It's not Travis Bingham—this guy's too old, too dark, more weathered-looking than the Travis I saw in this week's newspaper. He perches on the edge of the bench in front of the house and lights a cigarette. The man's wrinkled dress pants look flimsy, and I suspect the metal of the bench feels awfully cold through the thin fabric. He catches me staring at him and stares back. I wonder what he did to wind up there. Is he a murderer like Travis? A bank robber? A child molester? That last thought makes me a little nervous, and I start walking. Briskly, to beat the cold, or maybe to get away from the craggy old man smoking on the porch of the halfway house. I get down to the corner, turn right and head down the next street. It's a little after nine in the morning, and the neighborhood is slowly starting to come to life. People are shepherding kids with ice skates and hockey sticks out to cars, and I can see people through the windows of their houses watching Saturday-morning cartoons or making breakfast. I make another right turn, and another, a full trip around the block. The craggy man is gone when I pass the halfway house again. I suspect it's too cold to linger outside over a cigarette, even for a hard-core smoker.

I make another round of the block, and another. Even as bundled up as I am, I'm starting to feel the chill. My cheeks are burning. My toes are numb.

And then, on my fourth trip around the block, there he is. I can see him from a few houses away, perched in the other man's spot on the bench outside. He's wearing a coat that looks older than mine, a pair of ratty-looking jeans and the kind of mittens with the tops that flip open to turn them into a pair of fingerless gloves. I stop cold in my tracks—freezing cold, as a matter of fact, but too mesmerized to care. *He doesn't see me,* I realize, my heart pounding so hard I can feel it in my temples.

His hair is tidy—short and sandy, probably cut not too long ago—and his face has a shiny, freshly shaven look. He's shifting back and forth, maybe cold, maybe—what? Nervous? I shake my head. Nah. Couldn't be.

I take a few more steps, and then suddenly he's looking right at me. There's no way he doesn't know I'm staring at him. I can't look away. I've seen his picture hundreds, thousands, of times, and now here he is, four houses away, two houses away and now the length of a driveway from me.

He speaks. "Cold enough for ya?"

"Yeah." I can't believe he's talking to me. I can't believe I have nothing to say back to him but ridiculous small talk. His voice is higher than I thought it would be, more boyish than I expected. Somehow I figured he'd have a big, booming voice like the boogeyman I imagined he'd be.

"You look lost," he says.

"I…um…" Why can't I lie like Marie-Claire? I'm sure she'd have something smooth and convincing to say right now. "I'm…looking for the bus stop," I manage.

"Two blocks down, turn left." He smiles, tipping his head to one side a little to show me which way I should go. "There's a stop about three blocks over. I hope you don't have to wait too long in this weather."

"Okay. Thanks."

I linger for a second longer, my gaze locking with his for a second, and a shudder runs down my spine as I get a good look at those cold, yellow-green eyes of his. Only they don't hold that same killer stare I remember from the front page of the paper. They're…nothing. Not evil, not soulless, just…eyes.

"Stay warm," he calls as I turn and continue up the street, my hands clenched so tightly into fists inside my fuzzy mittens that I can feel them making half-moon fingernail marks on the insides of my palms.

* * *

I sit slumped on the backseat of the bus on the way up the Mountain to meet everyone. I had so much to say to Travis Bingham; how could I have just blanked out like that? It's all I've been thinking of the past two days, and I had a million things running through my head that just didn't come out of my mouth when I had the chance. I sniffle as the snot in my nose starts to thaw in the warmth of the bus, then peel off my gloves to expose fingers raw and red from the cold despite my fuzzy mittens.

I figure I was nervous this time. I wasn't sure what to expect when I met him, and even though I'd sent them away, I still felt a little like Katie and Griffin and Marie-Claire were standing over my shoulder while I talked to him.

"Next time," I hear myself say out loud. "Next time I'll do better." I look around, startled at the sound of my own voice, but no one is looking at me. People talking to themselves on the Hamilton Street Railway—which is the name of the bus company, not an actual railway— is not unusual, so I'm sure my mumblings are not too alarming to my fellow passengers. What's most startling to me, though, is how little thought I have to put into the idea that there's going to be a next time. I don't need to consult my posse—heck, I don't even think I'm going to *tell* them next time I pay Mr. Bingham a visit. I wasn't sure before, but now I know. This is something I need to do all by myself.

* * *

They're all halfway through their lunch by the time I join them at the food court. The three of them watch me intently as I wait in line at the Taco Bell and come back to the table with my burrito and Fries Supreme.

"So what happened?" Griffin asks through a mouthful of Chinese noodles.

I've been practicing this lie on the bus the entire way up the Mountain. I give him a casual shrug, look him right in the eye.

"Nothing." I slide into a chair. "I walked around the block a few times, but he never came out."

SUNDAY

There are twenty-four tiles on the ceiling in my mother's room. I spend a lot of time here, sitting in the plastic visitor's chair with my head tipped all the way back against the cinder-block wall, counting the little black flecks in each acoustic tile.

I love and hate Sundays in just about equal measure. First of all, I get to sleep in, which is great—unless Emily is just coming in from a night out and crashing around the room. And Simon sometimes cooks breakfast, which is also great. I love a hot breakfast: bacon, scrambled eggs, toast with peanut butter. That's what we had this morning, and it beats the hell out of a bowl of store-brand corn flakes, which is what I usually have on a school day.

Sunday-morning cartoons aren't great, but sometimes if Wex is busy playing with his Game Boy or something, I can find a cable channel playing reruns of *Happy Days* or *Alf* without him complaining too loud. *Alf* is a little stupid—it's funny enough, but I like to pretend I'm part of the family when I watch TV. Somehow I just can't picture myself living with a rude little alien, unless you count Wex.

But then, around ten thirty, the day starts to suck. The three of us—me, Wex and Simon—pile into the cab of Simon's beat-up pickup truck and head up the Mountain to see Momma.

It's a nice enough place she's in, I guess. The hallways are narrow and it always smells a little like pee, but she has her own room and the nurses are always okay to her, even when she's having one of her crazier-than-usual days. Momma's window doesn't look out on anything special; the building is U-shaped, and from her window all you can see is the courtyard in the middle of the U and the windows of rooms identical to hers on the other side of the building. But there's a little sitting room on the other side of the hall with an amazing view: you can see forever, all the way to Toronto on a clear day like this. The steel plants down by the harbor are spewing their usual filth into the sky, but they're far enough away from here that they look almost fake, like an ugly, dirty postcard. Some days they've got

Momma sitting in front of the windows in there, propped up in her wheelchair facing the TV, her watery gray eyes staring blankly at *The 700 Club* or *Dr. Phil* or whatever's on, and Wex and I spend the entire visit pretending to look at her while we stare out the window. I don't mind coming to visit on those days, when she's in the TV room. But today she's just stuck in her own room, staring at the walls, picking at the little balls of lint on her lap blanket. Simon is off somewhere talking to the nurse on duty about Momma's medication and whether she should go to physical therapy three times a week instead of just twice. Grown-up, responsible Simon. So Wex and I are stuck in here, trying to make conversation with my mother.

"It's supposed to snow this week," I tell her.

"That's nice." There's a long silence while I tip my head back and count the ceiling tiles again.

"Where is Simon?"

"He's out talking to the nurse. He'll be back in a few minutes."

"Okay. Who did you say you were again?"

* * *

My mother wasn't always like this, but she's been a little...off...for as long as I can remember. Simon says she managed to hold it together for a few years after my dad died, but my own memory of that time is understandably fuzzy. My most vivid memories of life with Momma consist of getting home from school to find her doing something bizarre, like sitting on the front porch naked with a screwdriver in her hand—that's a glass of vodka and orange juice, for the record, not a hand tool. Simon always said she was on so many different kinds of pills that it made her screwy. Some for her sore back, some to help her sleep at night, some to cheer her up, some to keep her from freaking out.

When I was nine and Wex came along, she managed to function well enough to keep him fed and changed when Emily couldn't be bothered, which was most of the time. Simon didn't live with us then—or rather, we didn't live with him. He had his own place and dropped by once or twice a week to help Momma pay her bills or mow the lawn.

And then there was a day when everything changed.

The bus got me home early that afternoon—not by much, maybe ten minutes. A couple of kids were absent from school that day, down with whatever flu was going around that season, and we didn't have to make the first two stops, so it was five after four instead of four fifteen when I got home. A bonus: I would only miss the first five minutes of *Who's the Boss?* on DejaView instead of half of it like I usually did.

I knew there was something wrong when I stepped inside the door. I could hear Wex—he was two at the time—screaming in his playpen, a hoarse, frantic sound like he'd been yelling for hours and nobody was answering. I went there first, picked him up and calmed him down. He was hyperventilating, taking great gasps of air, his whole body quivering as I held him.

"Wexy, Wexy, Wex. Shh, shh. Where's Grandma?"

"G-g-gamma," he managed, his cheeks stained with snot and tears.

I carried him upstairs, thinking I'd find her passed out on the bed. That had happened before, although I was surprised that Wex's screaming hadn't woken her.

"Mom?!" I alternated between rage and panic on the way upstairs—eleven-year-old me, furious that she would pass out and leave me to care for the screaming baby when I clearly had better things to do, like watch TV or go to Katie's house. But on the other hand, I couldn't shake the knot in the pit of my stomach, the feeling that something was horribly wrong. Where was my mother?

I set Wex down in the hallway and checked her bedroom: nothing. The bed was made; that was unusual.

The living room was tidier than usual, too, come to think of it. The rugs were vacuumed, the piles of laundry that usually littered the floors were tucked neatly away in the hampers, and the TV was off.

I wouldn't have thought to check the bathroom next if it weren't for the tiniest of sounds.

Bloop.

The tap dripped in our bathtub. That's important to know. It dripped all the time, leaving brown rust marks down the side of the bathtub. Simon kept promising he was going to come over and scrub the stains off. He'd been promising to fix the taps for more than a year, but he'd never gotten around to it. I was so used to the sound by then that I never noticed it anymore: *plonk, plonk, plonk* as the water drops hit the metal of the tub. But the sound that day was something different: the *bloop* of a drop of water falling into a full tub.

I froze for what may have only been a second or two in the bathroom doorway, watching the tiny ripples on the surface of the water and my mother's long dark hair floating to the surface, hiding her face.

I hauled my mother as far out of the tub as I could manage, leaving her draped over the side with her head hanging down as I bolted down the hall to her bedroom, where she kept the phone, my clothes soaked through and my heart racing so fast it felt like it was going to pump its way right out of my chest. The doctor at the hospital said if I'd been a few minutes later she wouldn't have made it, but as it was, she'd been out of air long enough that she'd never be right in the head again. Not that there was much right about her to begin with—at least, not that I remember.

Sometimes I think it might have been an accident: she just took too many pills and fell asleep in the tub. Mostly, though, I'm pretty sure she did it on purpose. I look in her eyes now, shiny and pale and as vacant as a doll's, and I wonder if there's maybe some part of her that's mad at me for coming home too early that day.

"Jenna? Do you think we can go out for lunch after this?" Wex is bored, and who could blame him? Talking to Momma is about as exciting as watching grass grow.

"Yeah, probably. We'll have to ask Simon."

"Where is Simon?" Momma asks again.

"I told you, Momma, he's outside talking to the nurse."

"That's good. Tell him to make sure they don't give me that tapioca anymore. It makes me gag."

"I'll tell him. I promise."

After a while Wex gets up and goes out in the hall to find Simon. Alone with my mother, I stare her down for a few moments as she stares into space. I wonder if there's anyone still in there.

"I saw him, you know, Momma. Travis Bingham. He's out of jail. I met him."

"Travis?"

"The guy who killed Daddy. Do you remember that?"

"Such a nice boy," says Momma.

"Who are you talking about? Daddy?"

"Travis. Such a nice boy."

I stare at my mother for a few minutes, trying to figure out what she's talking about.

"Mom, Travis Bingham is the man who killed Daddy. How can you forget that?"

She blinks, her pale eyes so much like my own but somehow...I don't know, lifeless. Dull.

"I'm sorry, who did you say you were again?"

I want to shake her, scream at her, want to make her understand that Travis Bingham is out roaming the streets again, ask her what I should do next. I wish I had the kind of mother I could ask for advice about things, but somehow I doubt that even at her most lucid Momma would have had any helpful advice on this subject.

After a few more minutes, Simon comes back in. He sits down by Momma's bed and puts his hands on hers.

"Hey, Ma. How's everything?"

"Simon, who is this?" Momma points at me, accusing. "Why is she in my room?"

"This is Jenna, Ma. Remember?"

"Don't be ridiculous. Jenna is a little girl."

And so it goes.

* * *

After we leave the nursing home, Simon drops me off in front of the used-CD store where Katie works. "Are you sure you're okay to walk home? It's minus forty with the windchill," he says. "It's Sunday. If you miss the bus, you're going to be stuck outside for an hour waiting for the next one."

"I'm fine. I'll get a ride with Katie's mom. She won't mind."

Not only will she not mind, she'll insist on driving me home and probably offer to buy me dinner on the way. I probably won't turn her down; I rarely do. It's not like Katie and her mom are exactly poster children for the average nuclear family, but after a visit with my mother, sometimes it's just nice to feel normal for an hour. I think that might be my favorite thing about Sundays.

Katie's sitting behind the counter, watching a DVD on the store TV. The place is tidy enough, but it has that musty old-building smell that seems to permeate most of the stores along this strip. She has the whole store to herself. There are no customers on Sunday afternoons at this time of year—Ottawa Street is deserted on cold days. There are occasional shoppers pulling up to one store or another and running in for a minute, but it's far too miserable out for browsing. The real soul of the street—the antique stores, consignment stores, the store where Katie works—is more or less asleep for the winter. It will come alive again in March or April when trendy shoppers who think *antique* is a verb will wander from shop to shop, looking for treasures.

Katie's a sucker for chick-flick romantic comedies the way I'm a sucker for eighties family sitcoms. Maybe that's because she thinks having a boyfriend is as unlikely for her as having a normal family is for me. She's watching something with Meg Ryan in it, with the volume on low so she can listen to music on her iPod at the same time.

I pull up a second chair behind the counter and sit beside her. "Any customers yet?"

"Yeah, one guy. Right when we opened. He was waiting outside to see if we have a copy of Ted Nugent's greatest hits."

"Who the hell is Ted Nugent, and why would you wait outside in this weather for his greatest hits?"

"Beats me. We didn't have it anyway, so I guess he's still out there looking."

Katie takes out her earbuds and turns up the volume on the movie.

"What are we watching?" I ask.

"*Prelude to a Kiss.* This young woman switches bodies with an old man on her wedding day."

"Why would she want to do that?"

Katie shrugs. "I think because she's got her whole life ahead of her and she's afraid it's going to suck. So she trades bodies with this dying old man because he's already lived his life, and he doesn't have anything else to worry about anymore. I don't really get it, myself."

"I do."

"Really?" She sounds astonished, which I try not to take as an insult. I guess it's not very often that I understand something and Katie doesn't.

"I really do. I'd trade places in a heartbeat with somebody who doesn't have anything left to worry about. It feels like I spend my whole life thinking about what awful thing is going to happen next."

"I know you do. Which is a shame, because it takes up all the time you should be spending actually having a life."

I wonder whether I should feel insulted by that or whether I should point out that Katie's life isn't exactly a laugh a minute either, but in the end I just lean back in the plastic chair behind the counter and try to watch the movie.

* * *

Katie's mom takes us out for supper at one of the new restaurants that was built after the old mall got torn down. I order a personal pizza—it's the cheapest thing on the menu, and much as I like getting free food, I don't want to wear out my welcome. I could buy my own dinner if I wanted to today—I still have a pocket full of money and no particular plans for it—but I'd rather save it, if I can, for when I really need it.

Griffin texts me halfway through supper: wane 2 coma ova? As technologically savvy as he is, Griffin has yet to master the finer points of both spelling and predictive text. We get Katie's mom to drop us off at his place, with promises that we'll be ready at nine thirty sharp for her to come and pick us up.

Griffin's dad is a university professor, and his mom is a nurse. They live in a brand-new two-story stucco house with an attached garage and a finished basement.

It sticks out like a sore thumb on a street full of ratty eighty-year-old bungalows in various states of disrepair. Or rather, I guess it would be more accurate to say it sticks out like a healthy thumb on a street full of broken fingers. Griffin's parents seem to think they're doing the neighborhood a favor just by living in it, like they're singlehandedly going to raise the property values of the entire street. They talk all the time about doing their part to make the East End a better place, but I'm not entirely sure what they mean by that. It's not like they're doling out food at the soup kitchen on their days off or anything. They don't even talk to their next-door neighbors except to tell them to move their garbage cans.

Griffin's dad meets us at the door in a golf shirt and khakis. He plasters on a smile. "Griff! Your friends are here, buddy."

Griffin's room is through the kitchen and living room and down the stairs. We hang up our coats in the front hall and shuffle past his mom. She's sitting in the kitchen in yoga pants and a T-shirt from some fundraising 10K race she ran last year, reading the *Toronto Star* and munching a rice cake with peanut butter.

"So nice to see you girls again. How is everything at school?" she says.

"Fine," we mumble in unison, and carry on down the plush-carpeted stairs to Griffin's domain. It's more of an apartment than a bedroom: he's got his own fridge, his own bathroom, every piece of electronics you could imagine and, best of all, a lock on the inside of his door. He bolts it as soon as we come in, like his parents might chase us downstairs to ask us more shallow, meaningless questions.

"Did my mom try to give you anything?" he asks me.

"Not today. We really didn't stop to chat though. She may get me on the way out."

Every time I see Griffin's mom, she offers me something: clothes, mostly, or old books. I guess she sees me as a convenient way to make a charitable contribution without even leaving the house.

"She'll probably offer you her winter coat," Katie says. She perches on Griffin's overstuffed chair. It has speakers built into it so his video games can be in surround sound. "His dad was giving you the hairy eyeball when you came in."

"I like that coat," I say. "It's warm. And it's got history. I like things with a story behind them."

Griffin takes the *Pöang* chair, which is stretched canvas over a plywood frame. It comes from IKEA, where every piece of furniture has a name. Half the stuff in

Griffin's room is from there. He can tell you his bed is a *Trondheim*, his dresser is a *Hemnes*, his bookshelf is a *Grevbäck*. "What's the story behind your brother's old coat then? It used to be his, and now it's not. So what? It's actually a little gross, if you want the truth. I don't get why you're so attached to it."

"I just like it. It reminds me of a simpler time."

"But…" Griffin trails off, frustrated. We've had this conversation before, and I've never been able to make him understand. "I just don't understand the appeal of being obsessed with the past. It's not like you can fix it. Why not be obsessed with the future instead? Plan what you're going to do once you get out of school, worry about your career. Settle down, have a kid or something. Get out of this hellhole of a city."

"Why is everybody suddenly so obsessed with my obsessions?" My voice gets a little shriller than I want it to. "Two days ago, you were all about pushing me to go see Travis Bingham and have some big showdown, and now you all want me to get over it and move on with my life?"

Griffin shrugs. "Well…we got to talking. Katie and Marie-Claire and me, while we were waiting for you up at the mall. We were really hoping you'd run into this Travis guy and get this all out of your system. I mean, don't get me wrong, you're awesome. But we all think it would be better for you if you just moved past this."

My eyes tear up suddenly, like I've just been slapped hard in the face. I look back and forth from Katie to Griffin, my two best friends in the world. Katie looks a little guilty, like she's ratted me out or something, but Griffin doesn't look a whole lot different than he always does: long-nosed and beady-eyed, with his eyebrows slightly arched like he's only mildly interested in whatever's going on.

"I'm really sorry if I can't just get over my entire life and move on," I shout, yelling so loud I can hear my voice bouncing off the ceramic tiles in Griffin's bathroom. "But since it seems to be a big deal all of a sudden, how about I just get over the two of you and move on?"

I stomp up the stairs, wishing the plush carpeting would allow me to make a louder, more dramatic exit. I slip my shoes on without untying them, stomping down the heels, then grab my coat from the rack in the front hall and carry it outside with me to put it on, slamming the door behind me.

Griffin's dad hears me from the living room and follows me out.

"Everything okay, Jenny?"

"My name is Jenna. And I'm afraid your son is a colossal asshole." I put up my hood, dig around in my pockets for my mittens. I can only find one, but I'm not about to go back in the house to look for it.

Griffin's dad looks perplexed. "Do you—can I—um… offer you a lift home?"

"I'm fine." It's cold enough that the tears in my eyes are freezing, making them sting. I put on my one mitten and stomp down the front steps to the driveway, turn right on the sidewalk and head home.

It takes longer than I thought it would to get there, and I'm switching my mitten back and forth from one hand to the other every few minutes so my fingers won't get too cold, but it doesn't do a lot of good.

I mumble under my breath, catching the eye of a little old man dragging his garbage can to the curb. He probably thinks I'm crazy and homeless, roaming around talking to myself on a night like this, because he keeps his eye on me as he heads back up to his porch, making sure I keep on walking past his house.

What kind of friends do I have, anyway? It's not like I can pick and choose, of course. Most kids take one look at me and either laugh or turn the other way. But I've spent most of my life hanging out with Griffin and Katie, putting up with all their faults and foibles; isn't that what friends do? So what if I'm fixated on what happened to my dad? It's better than being fixated on food, like Katie, or designer clothes, like Griffin. Isn't it?

* * *

"You don't look like you got a ride home."

"What?"

Simon's watching that TV show where a team of interior designers visits a family who has had some horrible crisis and builds them a new house. As if that's going to solve all their problems.

"I said you look like you just walked across half the city. You said you were getting a ride from Katie's mom."

I shrug. My nose is starting to run, and I wipe it on my mitten. "Katie and I had a fight."

"Well, you should have called me. I would have picked you up. That's why I pay for you to have a cell phone, dumbass."

"Go to hell." I drop my coat on the floor in the front hallway, too cold and lazy to hang it up.

"Pick up your jacket, you lazy slob. And then go have a bath. It'll warm you up."

I shoot him a dirty look but head for the bathroom anyway. A long soak will do me good, I suppose. At least it'll give me a chance to think things through.

Simon's show is over by the time I get out of the tub. I bundle up in my flannel pajamas with the flying sheep on them and sit with him to watch *Family Guy*. It's a cartoon, but it seems truer to me than that cheesy home-makeover show. People being nasty to each other is much more realistic than people doing huge, life-changing favors for strangers.

I can feel him staring at me as I watch, and during a commercial I turn to stare back. "What the hell is your problem?"

"Buck up, sad sack," he says. "I'm sure you and Katie will be back to best buddies first thing tomorrow."

I give him a kick. "Piss off."

"Suit yourself. That's what I get for trying to be nice."

MONDAY

I'm not even out of bed yet, but I can tell it's warmer out this morning. My bed is on the outside wall of the building, and the past few days it's been ice-cold to the touch despite my having the baseboard heaters turned up high. I'm sure Emily has been nice and toasty down on the bottom bunk, on the few nights she's actually been home, but somehow the warmth just doesn't reach all the way up to my bunk.

I ignore the alarm for a few minutes, but I can't fall back asleep; the clock radio is across the room, and I have to go all the way down the ladder to turn it off. I keep it set to a multilingual station, turned up loud. I don't know what language the announcers are speaking this morning, but I guess Italian. The DJ sounds like Giuseppe, the plumber Simon calls when there's a mess he can't fix. Some days it sounds like people speaking Arabic, or whatever language the terrorists speak in the war movies Simon likes to watch.

I take a shower, make a futile attempt to tame my shock of hair and head out the door, wondering if I'll have any friends left when I get to school. I decide to skip breakfast—there's still a knot in my stomach after my falling-out with Katie and Griffin last night, and somehow I'm just not in the mood to put anything else in there.

I don't see any of them when I get to school, but that's not unusual. Griffin and Katie have history first thing, and I have art. Marie-Claire's in art class with me, but she's not here this morning. Again, that's not unusual: she's late half the time anyway.

We sit at big tables like in kindergarten and wait for the morning announcements. The basketball team is on a winning streak. The hockey team lost its game on Friday. The math club—the only kids at school more bizarre than my little group—is meeting after school, new members are welcome. Mr. Hogan tells the boys at the table next to mine to take off their baseball caps while "O Canada" plays, but Nate Burke whines about hat head and Quinn Ross takes his off for "our home and native land" and then slips it back on again in time for the first "stand on guard for thee." Mr. Hogan lets it slide. Teachers let a lot of things slide with those two. It's got to be easier than actually trying to control them.

Marie-Claire slips in on the last notes of the anthem and takes her seat at my table—not beside me, where she usually sits, but kitty-corner, in the seat that usually sits empty.

"What's the matter, Frenchy, you don't want to be Canadian? Skipping 'O Canada'?" Nate throws an eraser at her, catching her in the shoulder. "You should just go back to Quebec and separate."

Without a thought, I jump to her defense. "She's from New Brunswick, you dumbass, not Quebec."

"What's the difference?"

I open my mouth to point out that New Brunswick is an entirely different province, but Mr. Hogan catches my eye and shakes his head before I can says anything.

*　*　*

After class Marie-Claire takes off like a greased pig, dodging through the hallways like she's trying to get away from an ax-wielding farmer. I'm not sure why; our lockers are side by side and we both have to stop at them before second period. I catch up to her as she's working the combination on her lock: 20-43-16, for the record.

"So nobody's speaking to me now?"

Marie-Claire shrugs. "Look, Jenna, I just don't want to choose sides. I don't have so many friends at this school to start with, and if half of them suddenly don't want to talk to me—"

"So the majority rules, then?"

"I guess so. Look, I'm sorry. Maybe if you just apologized to Griffin and Katie...he says you told his dad Griffin's an asshole."

"Well, he was being one, so I guess I'm not sorry for saying it. Not much point in apologizing if I'm not sorry." I unlock my locker and pull out the embroidered draw-string bag I keep my gym clothes in. Marie-Claire grabs her math book and goes upstairs to her next class, her head tucked into her chest as she hustles toward the stairs.

I sling the gym bag over my shoulder and head off to phys ed. Apologize to Griffin and Katie? Not a chance. I'm not even completely sure what we're fighting about, but I do know for sure I'm nowhere near done being mad.

I'm sure most of the kids who don't fit in spend their days in fear of phys ed class. It can be a scary ordeal if you're not one of the skinny, athletic, popular kids. I was one of the first kids in my class to need a bra, so I've always gotten my fair share of snide comments and rude stares, but now that most of the other girls have caught up to me, it's less of a big deal. Gym in general has always been ten times worse for Katie than it is for me—not just the changeroom and, worse, the showers, but the whole process: getting picked last for teams, getting laughed at when she runs, standing in the corner when we're doing gymnastics, hoping nobody will notice she hasn't taken her turn to do a somersault because she can't make her body roll up in a little ball.

Today we're practicing basketball shots, which would be tolerable if I was partnered with Katie. There are six basketball hoops in the gym and twenty-four of us in the class, which means four people practicing shots on each hoop. Ordinarily, Katie and I would just pair up with a couple of the other losers and hide in a corner for the entire class, pretending to take shots while we talked about whatever we were going to do after school. It would be the perfect day in gym class, really. We wouldn't even have to work up enough of a sweat to have to deal with the showers afterward, which is its own special kind of hell.

But today Katie pairs up with Imogene, a special-needs kid who takes gym with us. She's a nice kid, I guess, although her conversational subjects are pretty much limited to whatever shows are popular on the Disney Channel this month. I doubt whether even the six-year-olds in Wex's class still think Miley Cyrus is cool, but Imogene sure does. She's got about ten different Hannah Montana T-shirts, not to mention an assortment of bracelets, earrings and pins that she's not allowed to wear in gym class. I guess Katie prefers hearing about what happened on Disney yesterday to talking with me today. I don't even try to make conversation; she's clearly trying to freeze me out.

"I guess I'm stuck with you, huh?"

I feel my stomach tie itself in a little knot. I recognize that voice even without turning around: Ashley Walsh. She went out with Ned Street for a while last year, which is bad enough on its own, but she's been pretty nasty to me in her own right as far back as I can remember. In third grade, she used to climb up on the toilets in the school bathrooms and look at me over the stall walls while I was peeing. Last semester, when I'd finished reading a poem out loud in English class, she tripped me on the way back to my seat, then giggled and gave this big-eyed, innocent stare to the teacher, who looked up from his desk long enough to tell me to watch where I was walking. I guess it's easier to blame the weird kid than yell at the cool one.

I look Ashley over. She's wearing Lululemon pants and a tank top two sizes too small that shows off her cleavage. I'm pretty sure the next hour will be filled with snide comments about my old running shoes and worn-out Walmart sweatpants, and Ashley "accidentally" firing the ball at my head when I'm not looking.

I shake my head. "No thanks."

Ashley's neatly plucked eyebrows shoot up under her carefully fluffed bangs. "Excuse me?"

"I'm okay, thanks. I don't really want to be your partner."

I can actually see her getting mad. She starts turning pink around the ears, and her chest puffs out even farther.

"Well, I don't know who you're going to be partners with then. Your fat friend is all cozy with the retard over there, and we're the only two left."

It hits me then: something is amiss. Like there's a disturbance in The Force. Why isn't Ashley off with the rest of her crowd? Megan and Jessica and Emily, her usual gang, are off in a corner with Victoria Harper, who is usually nothing more than a hanger-on but today looks like a full-fledged member of the club. They're standing around the hoop in the middle of the gym, shoulder to shoulder, with Megan and Emily each clutching a basketball like they're about to take a shot, but it's mostly a ruse in case Ms. Robbins looks over while they're chatting. Every once in a while Victoria glances back over her shoulder to see if Ashley's still talking to me. Then she gives me a creepy little sneer and turns back to the rest of the gang.

"Miss Walsh, Miss Cooper: mixing it up today, are we?" Ms. Robbins was born to be a gym teacher. She has about fifteen different tracksuits in every color of the rainbow, and an office wall full of motivational posters with pictures of sweaty people making great tennis serves, running across finish lines, sinking baskets. She's the kind of person who actually says things like "No pain, no gain" and "Winners never quit, quitters never win" with a straight face.

As soon as she comes over, Ashley plasters on her big, fake, doe-eyed smile. "Ms. Robbins, it looks like Jenna and I are the last two without partners."

"There's an easy solution to that, don't you think?" She claps us both on the shoulders like we're all good buddies. "Come on, girls. Let's work up a sweat here."

"Whatever you say, Ms. Robbins," Ashley says.

I trudge over to the wire bin that has a few lifeless basketballs left at the bottom and retrieve the one that has the least amount of give when I poke it. Ashley examines her fingernails, chewed to the quick, while I make my way back across the gym.

"So, what's going on with you and Fatty?" She takes the ball from me, gives it a bounce.

"Her name's Katie." She and I may be on the outs, but it's still pretty low to pick on Katie's weight.

"Whatever. What's going on? I thought you two were besties."

I shrug. "A difference of opinion, I guess. What's the story with your little club?"

Ashley's right eye twitches a little, like she's irked that I noticed. "The same thing, I guess."

"All right. So I guess that makes us partners."

She passes me the ball, a little harder than she really needs to, and I toss it halfheartedly at the basket. It goes right through the middle of the hoop, nothing but net, like I'm some kind of athlete.

Ashley's carefully waxed eyebrows rise in surprise. "Not bad," she says.

* * *

After class I shower in about thirty seconds flat, then race to the cafeteria to sit at our regular table before everybody else gets there. Katie always finds some reason to hang back in gym class until everyone else has gone before she gets in the shower, and Griffin is in biology class, upstairs at the other end of the school. Marie-Claire gets there a few minutes after I do, shoots me a peeved look and finds another table. Everybody else shows up shortly afterward, glancing at me before they join her.

I dig my English book out of my satchel and pretend to read. Every once in a while I look over at my so-called friends. Griffin is laughing too loud, like he wants to make sure I notice how much fun they're having without me. I'm sure they're making plans for later and talking about what a loser I am, sitting over here by myself.

So this is what it's like to get frozen out. I can't say I recommend it.

* * *

After school it starts to snow a little—big fluffy globs that look pretty drifting through the air but start to look dingy and slushy the second they hit the ground. It's warm enough for me to take the kids to the park and let them run off some steam while I sit on the picnic bench and make sure nobody falls off the top of the climber.

Wex sits beside me, watching the other kids play. I don't bother asking him why he doesn't join in; the other kids are about as keen on him as my peers are on me. We sit for an hour or so, Wex up on the picnic table and me on the bench, neither one of us saying much of anything, until my butt is frozen from the cold metal. Finally I stand up and do a little wiggle to get the feeling back in my upper thighs.

"All right, guys. Time to go."

There's some moaning and whining from Xavier, the oldest of my charges, but most of them are starting to get a little chilled. The snow isn't really sticking around, and the sun is starting to sink behind the escarpment. We march back home in a line, with me and Wex bringing up the rear, and Xavier way up ahead like he's too cool to be seen with all these little kids.

"Slow down, Xavier. You're too far away."

He heaves his shoulders, turns around with his hands thrown in the air. "Come on. You're too slow. You said it was time to go home, so let's *go.*"

But instead of speeding up, I stop in my tracks. Rounding the corner ahead of us, coming right toward us, is Ashley Walsh, resplendent in her bright pink down jacket and Ugg boots.

"Funny seeing you north of Main Street," I say, trying to sound casual. She's clearly looking for me, because she slows when she sees me. I wonder if she's going to beat me up as punishment for some offense I might have committed in gym class…or maybe just to cleanse herself from the humiliation of having been seen with me in public at school.

"I heard you'd be around here. Scott Becker says he sees you here all the time."

"I usually am after school, if the weather's okay."

She turns around and falls into step beside me. I have no clue what she's after. She's a little shorter than I am, maybe ten pounds lighter. I'm pretty sure I could take her in a fight, and I don't think she'd jump me in front of a crowd of little kids anyway. I wonder if they'd all spring to my defense, and I smile a little at the thought of Ashley getting her ass kicked by a bunch of first-and-second-graders.

"What are you smirking about?" she wants to know.

I shrug. "Nothing special. So, what brings you to my neck of the woods?"

"I was thinking after gym class. You're not so bad."

"Gee, thanks."

"No, I mean, seriously. You're really weird. I mean, like, freak-show weird. But you're kind of funny, too. Maybe we can hang out or something."

I stop in my tracks and stare at her. "Seriously? You spend ten years treating me like something you'd scrape off the bottom of your shoe, and now we're buddies all of a sudden?"

Ashley shrugs. "Yeah. Sorry about that. But I figure… your friends aren't talking to you, my friends aren't talking to me…and it sucks having nobody to sit with at lunch."

"Is this some elaborate setup where you're going to spend a couple of weeks pretending to be my friend, then set me on fire in the cafeteria or something?" Wex looks up at me, alarmed. Sometimes I forget he's there, always listening. I ruffle his hair. "Don't worry, Wexy. Nobody's gonna do that." I shoot Ashley a pointed look. "Are they?"

Ashley looks genuinely bewildered. "No. I just thought…"

"We're going to my house," I tell her. "You can come along if you want, I guess."

I herd the kids into the vestibule of our apartment building, unlock the inside door and walk down the hall. Ashley's face is pinched, like she's afraid to touch anything with her hands.

"So this is where you live," she says, trying to sound like it's no big deal.

I nod and open the apartment door. "You don't have to be polite about it. I know it's a hole."

"No, it's not that bad. I mean, I'm sure it's…"

I don't get to find out where she's going with that train of thought, though, because Xavier's mother is waiting in our living room to pick him up. Remarkably, she has the rest of the money she owes me, which is up to forty bucks now. I tuck it in the back pocket of my jeans and mumble a thank-you. Out of the corner of my eye, I see Ashley taking in the room, casting a critical eye on the cluttered living room, the kitchen sink full of dirty dishes. I imagine her home is something out of *Good Housekeeping*, with spotless rooms painted in subtle earth tones, tidy afghans folded neatly over the backs of chairs, shelves covered in beautifully arranged knickknacks and wicker baskets full of magazines.

We sit in the living room, me on the couch and Ashley perched on the edge of the tattered La-Z-Boy chair like she's afraid it will swallow her whole if she sits back.

"So this is what you do every day, huh? Watch other people's kids?"

"Yeah." I suddenly realize I know nothing about this tidy pink Barbie doll sitting in my living room. "Do you have a job?"

"No. My dad thinks it would distract me from getting good grades. I just get an allowance for doing chores."

"Must be nice."

"What, getting an allowance?"

"Well, yeah. That and having a dad."

Ashley gives me a knowing look. "Ah, your parents are divorced."

"No, dead." I pause for effect, enjoying the look of horror on her face for a second before I elaborate. "My dad is, anyway. My mom is…sick. She's in a nursing home."

"Wow. No wonder you're so screwed up. No offense."

"You know, just saying 'no offense' as soon as you say something rude doesn't mean it wasn't offensive."

Ashley looks startled and thinks that over for a minute. "Yeah, I guess you're right. Sorry." It doesn't make up for nine years of her treating me like crap, but I suppose it's a start.

"You want something to eat or drink or something?" I'm not much of a host. It's not like I have a huge variety of guests over. Griffin and Katie and Marie-Claire all know where the food is and help themselves if they're hungry. *Helped* themselves, I suppose.

"Yeah, I could eat," Ashley says.

I look in the cupboard, find Twinkies and grape juice. Wex comes in and wants some, then plunks himself down in front of the tv to watch *Phineas and Ferb*.

Ashley makes a face. "Ugh. Kid stuff. My little sister watches this all the time."

"You want to go sit in my room instead?"

I regret the words as soon as they're out of my mouth. I can't let Ashley Walsh see my bedroom, with Rubbermaid boxes of yarn lining one wall and Emily's posters of thrash metal bands tacked to another. I realize I don't even know whether Emily is home. Griffin and Katie are used to finding her passed out on the floor, the couch, wherever she happens to land, but how do I explain her to someone like Ashley?

"Yeah. You have a TV in your room?"

"No, but I've got a little portable DVD player with a screen. Maybe we can watch a movie or something."

I lead the way to the bedroom, holding my breath a little as I open the door and hoping Emily is somewhere else. I relax a little as I see her bed is empty, although she's clearly been through here today, because it looks like a tornado hit.

"I share the room with my sister. It's a little messy."

"That's fine. You should see my room. My mom keeps threatening to go through with a garbage bag and throw everything out."

"My mom never really cared much. And my brother doesn't care at all, really."

"Really? You live with your brother? That's so weird. What happened to your dad, anyway?"

So suddenly I'm pouring out my entire life story to Ashley Walsh, who perches on the edge of Emily's bed and leans forward with her eyes bugging out like this is the most fascinating thing she's ever heard. Before I stop to think about what I'm saying, I've told her everything— even the part I didn't tell Katie and Griffin and Marie-Claire: my meeting with Travis Bingham.

Ashley's mouth is agape. "That. Is. So. Cool."

"Cool?"

"Seriously. I mean, who knew you were so, you know, *deep*. I just thought you were this weird kid who hangs out with losers and knits in the library. Look at you, tracking down killers and junk."

I shrug. "Well, it wasn't the way I wanted it to go. I was hoping for something a little more...satisfying. And now none of my friends are talking to me because they think I'm totally obsessed with ancient history."

"Well, I think it's really interesting. And your friends suck if the stuff that's important to you isn't important to them."

I look Ashley over carefully. She might be trying to put one over on me, but she seems so earnest, it really seems like she might be sincere.

"So why are your friends shutting you out all of a sudden?" I ask her. "I thought you were all pals for life."

"Oh, it's stupid." Her voice breaks a little. "You know I used to go out with Ned Street, right?"

"That was kind of hard to miss. You were always making out in the halls."

"Yeah, well." She shifts a little, looks away like she's embarrassed. "Well, he started sneaking around with Carrie Lerner behind my back, and when I found out about it she started this rumor that I was pregnant and got an abortion, even though Ned and I never even, you know, *did it,* and so I got mad and told Maddie Grant that Carrie was the one who—"

The story goes on for a while, and, I have to admit, I lose track of who said what to whom and sort of drift off a little in my head. It all boils down to someone making up stories about someone else, lies piling up on top of lies and poor Ashley landing squarely on the bottom of the heap. I really do wind up feeling a little sorry for her in the end, even though I haven't completely followed the chain of events. I just nod sympathetically and throw in a "Really? That's terrible" every once in a while, kind of like I do when I'm listening to Henry or Wex ramble on and on about something. I wonder if this is how Katie and the rest of them feel when I talk about Travis Bingham.

"So then Ned said he didn't even want to be friends with me anymore, and now none of them are even talking to me."

"Wow. That sucks."

"Yeah."

There's a long silence, and I can see Ashley looking around the room, taking it all in. Her eyes keep going back to the clear Rubbermaid containers full of yarn and knitting patterns.

"So you really know how to knit?" she finally says. "I mean, I've seen you in school, but…you look like you're really serious about it with all this stuff."

"Yeah. My mom taught me when I was seven. Before she was really, um, sick."

"So all those weird sweaters and hats and stuff you wear…you make them all?"

"Yeah."

"That's so cool. Seriously. I mean, I always thought you just got them at the Goodwill or something, but you actually…like, you're some kind of *artist* or something."

I shrug. "I guess. I never really thought that much about it."

We chat for a few more minutes before Simon knocks on the door and yells through it that he's brought home KFC.

"No need to yell. You can open the door," Ashley yells back. "We're not naked or anything." And she giggles madly, but I don't really get the joke.

Simon opens the door, pokes his head around. "Hmm. I don't know you. When Wex said Jenna had a friend over, I just figured it was Katie or Elvira."

I throw a book at him. *The Chrysalids*. It bounces off his head, but it's a paperback so it probably doesn't hurt him too much. "Her name's Marie-Claire, you loser. And this is Ashley."

"Is Ashley staying for dinner?"

"Ashley could, if she's invited," she says with a big smile. Ye gads, is she *flirting* with my brother? Ew. What is it with people trying to flirt with Simon? It's not like he's terrible-looking, I guess, it's just…strange. And it's not like he even seems to notice. Besides, he's almost eighteen years older than we are, which is just gross.

Simon cocks an eyebrow. "Well, Ashley and Jenna should wash up, because dinner is going to be on the table in about two minutes, and Wex has been known to put away half a bucket of chicken on his own."

He closes the door behind him, and Ashley claps me on the shoulder like we're the best of friends. "Your brother's *cute*."

"He's thirty-two."

"Well, for an old guy, I mean. I don't want to *do* him or anything, but he's kind of weirdly adorable. Does he have a girlfriend?"

"Nope. Not for as long as I've known him."

"That's weird."

I shrug. I'd never thought of it as weird before that Simon doesn't go out on dates. He doesn't go out with friends either. He doesn't do much of anything, as a matter of fact. He's just…here.

* * *

Ashley is charming and animated over dinner, like she's part of the family. She makes a big show of playing with Wex, pretending to steal his nose even though he's really too old for that game, but Wex eats it right up, giggling and trying to grab her hand. Afterward she plunks herself down on the couch with us to watch TV—just makes herself right at home.

"So what's there to do around here at night?" she wants to know.

I shrug. "I usually watch TV and knit. Or go over to Katie's. That's pretty much it. What do you do at night?"

"Hang out. Go to the park or the mall or something."

We sit for a few minutes, staring at the TV. Ashley takes the remote control and flips through the channels, but there's nothing on worth watching.

"Hey, you want to see something?" I say finally.

"What's that?"

Simon is busy helping Wex get his pajamas on and his teeth brushed, and I know that as soon as Wex is in bed, Simon is going to flop out on the couch for the evening. I dig in the pocket of his jacket and pull out a huge wad of keys. I stuff them in the pocket of my hoodie, holding them tight so they don't jingle and attract Simon's attention.

"Let's go downstairs. You were asking about the guy who killed my dad; I want to show you something."

I'm feeling oddly nervous as I lead Ashley down the hall to the stairs. I've taken Katie down here before, but never anyone else. I feel like a pirate showing the new cabin boy where I've stashed the treasure chest.

I've never been in a medieval dungeon, but I imagine it would look a lot like the room in our basement where the storage lockers are. They're old-school creepy, with slatted wooden doors padlocked shut, packed with piles of musty boxes, artificial Christmas trees and bicycles in varying states of decay. There are a few empty lockers, and I always picture some emaciated guy inside, banging on the slats with a tin cup.

Ashley looks a little jumpy. "You're not bringing me down here to lock me in one of these cages to get back at me for being mean to you or something, are you?"

"I hadn't planned on it." Hmm. That almost sounded like an apology. "I just thought you might like to see this."

I pull Simon's keys out of my pocket and shuffle through them until I find the little brass key that opens our storage locker. It's full of stuff from our old house—furniture that wouldn't fit in the apartment, Rubbermaid containers full of my mom's old clothes, cardboard banker's boxes stuffed with old papers. I open up the one on top and pull out a file folder of old newspaper clippings.

"This is the guy who killed my dad."

"Wow." Ashley flips through the folder, skims the articles. "That's pretty amazing. Look at this—your name's in here, like, a hundred times. You're famous!"

"Yeah, for about six months, when I was born. And look how far it's gotten me. Besides, having everybody feel sorry for you isn't the same as being famous."

"Oh, come on. You're actually pretty all right, you know."

"Thanks. You're different than I thought you were too."

Ashley hands the folder back to me and opens up another box. "What's in this one?"

"I think that's Simon's old yearbooks and stuff."

"Really? What was he like in high school? I bet he was a hottie."

"How would I know? I was hardly even born when he graduated."

Ashley pulls out a blue hardcover book with gold embossed lettering and flips through it. "Look at these haircuts. All the girls look like that chick from *Friends* and the guys look like they're trying to be George Clooney on *ER*."

I take the book from her and flip through it, looking for a picture of Simon. "Here he is. On the basketball team."

"Ooh, a jock. Let me see. Was he cute?"

"Dude, he's my *brother*."

Ashley laughs. "I know. Just curious." She looks over my shoulder. "Wow. He looks so different. Look how skinny he is. I mean, not like he's fat now, just not as... bony. He looks better now."

"You are too weird." I flip through more pages. I don't bother to buy the yearbooks at my school. With only three people in my social circle to sign them, it hardly seems worth it. But it looks like Simon was a pretty popular guy: on nearly every page, somebody has proclaimed what a great friend he was, promised to get together over the summer, scribbled the same dirty limericks I still see scrawled on desks and bathroom walls at school now. I guess some art forms are just timeless.

Suddenly Ashley snatches the book out of my hands and slams it shut.

"You know what we should do tomorrow?"

So apparently we're a *we* now. "What's that?" I ask.

"We should totally cut school and get you a makeover." She looks me over thoughtfully. "How much money do you have?"

"A little. Why?"

"Perfect. We're *so* going shopping. Your wardrobe needs an update. And when was the last time you had a haircut?"

I run my hands over my braid, frizzy from that afternoon's snowfall. "I don't know, when I was ten, maybe?"

Ashley laughs. "That's like, what, six years?"

"Five and a half, I guess. Maybe longer. Maybe I was nine."

"Great. Then it's decided. I'll meet you here; we'll hit up the clearance racks at Limeridge. That should give us a good start. And we're getting your hair done.

I know a place you can get it done for eight bucks, and they actually do a pretty good job."

"Um, I..." I mull it over. I've never skipped school before. I mean, I've missed days when I was sick, and I did leave early once last semester when Wex fell on the playground at his school and split his lip open and the principal couldn't get hold of Simon or Emily. But to full-out take a day off without permission—that's just not something that's ever occurred to me. It's not like I think Simon will freak out, or even notice, for that matter, it's just...naughty. It's something Emily would do, but not good old, reliable Jenna. And for something as shallow and superficial as shopping for clothes? I can't help but wonder what Ashley's angle is. Is she dressing me up so she won't be embarrassed to be seen with me at school? Or is it something more sinister: is she planning to pick out clothes that are just out of style enough to earn me more mocking from her old gang?

Still, maybe this is the kind of thing one does when one has friends who aren't all charter members of the Loser Club. I toss the yearbook back in the banker's box and put the lid back on.

"Sure," I say finally. "Let's do that."

TUESDAY

As I braid my hair in the morning, I feel a nervous twinge. Do I really want to do this? I can hear Katie's voice in my head, telling me not to sell out, not to pretend to be someone else for the sake of having a new friend. But since I don't have any old friends left, what's the point of holding on to old habits? I do look scruffy. I've always chalked it up to my own personal style, but in truth I've never really put much thought into how I look, and I've never thought much of people who do. But who knows? Maybe if I look better, people will treat me better.

Simon is helping Wex with the zipper on his coat when I get out to the living room, and I dive past him and out the door without saying a word. It's not that I think he'll be mad about my skipping school; it's just that I don't want to have a conversation about it right now. I'm feeling conflicted enough as it is.

Ashley is waiting outside the building, dangling a set of car keys in her hand.

"We're taking my dad's car," she says. "We just have to walk down and pick it up from his work. He's working a twelve-hour shift. All we have to do is make sure we get it back before he gets off work at seven tonight."

"Oh. We'll have to be back before that—I have to pick up the kids from the bus."

"Really? You do that every day?"

"Rain or shine."

It's neither rain nor shine today. The sky is cloudy and ominous, and I wonder whether we might get that snowstorm Griffin was talking about the other day. The weather feels strangely appropriate, like the sky is angry at us for doing something wrong.

Ashley's dad works at one of the steel plants, and as we walk she chatters about how important his job is, how hard he works, how much money he makes. We wander down to the bottom of Ottawa Street, under a huge green metal building suspended over the road. It's like another world down here. Huge coil carriers, twenty-four-wheeled trucks loaded up with six massive coils of steel apiece, slog by us on the slushy roads.

From the way Ashley is talking, I'd have expected her dad to drive a Mercedes or something, not a dumpy old Ford that smells of cigarettes and greasy fast-food wrappers, but it's better to have a ride than take the bus on a day like this.

I fasten my seat belt as Ashley makes a big show of adjusting the mirrors.

"When did you get your license?" I ask.

"I haven't got it yet. But I took driver's ed last semester and I've got my G1."

"Don't you have to have your G2 to drive alone?"

"Yeah, but I'm not alone." Ashley grins. "I've got you."

"Um, you know I'm only fifteen, right?"

"That's fine. If we get pulled over, you're nineteen and left your license at home, okay?"

My heart is racing. This is now officially the wildest thing I've ever done. "Nineteen. Okay then."

We get to the mall just as the doors are opening, sales-clerks rolling open the metal doors and pushing racks of stuff out into the aisle.

"All right." Ashley rubs her hands together with a gleam in her eye. "We need a game plan. How much money do you have to spend?"

WHATEVER DOESN'T KILL YOU

I shrug. "Like, a hundred bucks."

"Whoo. All right, that's not much, but we'll make do." She looks me up and down. "What are you, a size eight? Ten?"

"I have no idea."

"All right, we'll figure it out."

It's clear that Ashley sees shopping as some kind of competitive sport. At the first store we come to, she grabs me by the hand and pulls me past racks of the newest styles—thirty-dollar blouses and fifty-dollar sweaters— and back to the clearance racks. And she's got some mad skills, too, plunging her arm elbow-deep into the mass of marked-down sweaters and pants and coming out with a bright blue T-shirt marked down from $17.99 to $3. She looks strangely triumphant, like a picture I once saw of a bear who'd just yanked a big salmon out of the river.

"This would look awesome with your hair color," she tells me. "You're *so* trying this on."

"Um, okay." I start to head off to the changeroom, but Ashley stops me.

"Are you kidding? We're getting more than that." And she proceeds to load me up. Again and again she plunges into the mass of clothes, coming up with a pair of jeans for $6, a sweater for $7.50, a skirt for $2.99.

I feel like a Barbie doll as she shoves me into change-room after changeroom, nodding approvingly or clucking her tongue if the neckline isn't quite right or the butt is too baggy. And remarkably, the mirror in the changeroom tells me she's right: it does feel pretty good to stare back at myself in a blouse that fits, a pair of pants without holes, a hoodie that actually makes me look like I have a figure. By the time I'm down to my last twenty dollars, I've actually managed to amass a decent wardrobe.

"It's too bad we couldn't find you a coat," Ashley says, "but next time you get paid, we'll get you one."

I'm exhausted from the marathon shopping spree, but oddly enough I'm beginning to understand that look of victory on Ashley's face when she digs into a pile of clothes and magically pulls out something that looks good. Still, I've never been dressed and undressed so many times in one day, and it's a bit of a relief to be back in my old clothes again at the end of the shopping spree. My relief is short-lived, though, as Ashley steers me toward the washrooms near the top of the escalator.

"Just so you know, we're throwing those out," Ashley says, pointing at my jeans. She grabs my shopping bags and puts them down on the counter by the sinks, then roots through my haul of clothes until she finds a green sweater and a pair of new jeans. "Put these on."

It's snowing when we get outside, and Ashley does a cursory job of brushing off her dad's car. I get in and buckle my seat belt, my stomach rumbling a little.

"So, um, is there a plan for lunch somewhere in the middle of my big makeover?"

"There's a great place to eat right across from the hairdresser's. We can get a shawarma or something afterward."

"Great." I don't know what a shawarma is, but it sounds exotic, like something trendy and sophisticated people might eat, and with my stylish—albeit 80 percent off—new wardrobe, I guess I can pretend to be trendy and sophisticated for an afternoon.

The hair salon is a dingy little place with the prices posted on a whiteboard in the window—men's and kids' haircuts $5, women's $8. It's freezing inside the shop, and there's only one other customer, an old woman in a parka with tinfoil patches all over her head. She's reading a copy of *InStyle* magazine that looks to be about two years old, judging from the dog-eared pages.

"I help you?"

The hairdresser is a terrifying little woman, Eastern European and nearly as wide across as she is tall. I take a step backward, but Ashley's right there, shoving me forward. "My friend needs a haircut."

"Okay. Sorry for the heat is broken. I waiting for the man to come fix."

"That's fine," I tell her. I leave my coat on and sit in the chair. The woman wraps me in a cape that fastens around my neck so tightly I can barely talk, then pulls out the elastic bands holding my braid in place. She starts roughly brushing out my hair, jerking my head back as she sorts out the curls.

"How you want your hair?"

"Um, I don't really know. Just…something nice, I guess. Something different."

The woman smiles, showing off a mouth full of crooked teeth that all look like they belong to different people.

"Okay. I take good care of you."

She sets at my head like a predator, armed with a spray bottle of water and a pair of scissors, spraying and hacking and spraying and hacking. I see huge chunks of reddish-gold curls falling to the floor, and despite myself I can feel my eyes brimming with tears. I remember my last haircut: some high-end place my mom took me to on a "girls' day out" where the lady cut my hair so short I looked like Little Orphan Annie.

"Don't make it too short, okay?"

"Is okay." The lady pats me on the shoulder. "I make your hair look nice."

Ashley hovers like a bumblebee, telling me how great I'm going to look when all this is over. I feel a lump welling in my throat. I guess I'm not very good with new things after all. Even when the old things suck, at least you know what to expect from them.

But after an eternity of spritzing and snipping and hair-pulling, I have to admit, my hair looks a lot better than it did—pretty good, in fact. Sort of a wavy bob that falls to my jawline. I look down at the floor and see mountains of orange fluff piled all around, but when I look back to the mirror, it doesn't seem to matter as much.

"That's so amazing," Ashley chirps. "Look, it changes the whole shape of your face. You look so hot."

I nod, my eyes misting up a little for no reason that I can discern. "Yeah. It looks pretty good."

The little European woman takes the cape off me like she's revealing a sculpture, and I stare at myself in the mirror, mesmerized. Ashley steps in and fluffs my hair, grinning. "Look at you! You're gorgeous!"

I don't even register the sound of the door chime ringing until I hear the hairdresser speaking to the two men who've stepped inside.

"You come about the heat?" she says.

"Yeah. What seems to be the problem?"

She sounds a little peevish. "I don't know. I pay you to find that out."

I look up to see who she's talking to—two guys in brown coveralls with their names embroidered on the pockets—and I can feel my stomach dropping as I realize who's standing there. The older man is fiftyish, balding, a clipboard tucked under his arm; the younger, thirtyish and dreadfully, heart-stoppingly familiar. There, in his coverall and grubby work boots and carrying a toolbox, is Travis Bingham.

I let out a little gasp and Ashley looks at me, puzzled. "What's the matter?"

"That's him," I say between gritted teeth. My heart is racing in my throat. I can feel my hands shaking.

"That's who?"

"Travis Bingham." She gives me a blank stare. "The guy who killed my dad."

"No way!" she says too loudly.

"Shh!" I duck so that she's between me and Travis. I don't want him to see me right now—not that he'd have the faintest clue who I am anyway.

"Well, you should say something."

"I don't know what to say. I'm not ready for this. I wasn't expecting to see him."

"Eight dollar."

"What?"

The hairdresser has her hand out. "Eight dollar. See, I tell you I make your hair look nice. You like it?"

"I—yes. I do. I like it." I dig through my pockets for change and find a crumpled five-dollar bill and a handful of coins.

"You have beautiful hair. You come back again, few months. No wait so long next time to get cut, okay?"

"Sure. Okay. I will. I mean, I won't."

And away she goes to talk to Travis and the older guy, who looks like he's probably the boss, about the heat. I duck outside with Ashley at my heels.

"Well, are you going to talk to him or what?"

"I—I'm not ready. I don't know what to say."

"Well…" She pulls her cell phone out of her pocket and checks the time. "Why don't we go get something to eat and we can think about it? Then when they're done whatever they're doing, we can come back and meet them outside."

I think about the last time I stalked Travis Bingham with a gang of people. "No. I think I really need to be alone to talk to him."

"Really?" Ashley looks shocked. I don't know if she's more surprised by the idea of my confronting Travis on my own or the thought of doing *anything* alone. It occurs to me that I've never seen her without an entourage before.

Having only me to hang around with must be absolutely killing her.

I decide that what Ashley needs is a project. That will make her feel like she's involved without actually bringing her along with me. "Can you do me a favor? I need to find out where he works."

She brightens at that. "You want me to go back in and ask him?"

"No!" I can just see Ashley opening her mouth and spilling the whole story. "How about…you go in and see if the name of the company is printed on their uniforms or something. Distract the hairdresser—ask her how much it would cost to get highlights or…I don't know. Just make something up. But see if they've got an address or a phone number or something. That way I can go find him at work. But not today. Today I'm not ready."

With a job to do, Ashley ducks back into the store, and I stand outside on the sidewalk. The snow will look dingy and gray tomorrow, filled with flecks of the coal dust that is always floating through the air in this end of town, but right now the fat white flakes against the gray of the old buildings look dreamy, otherworldly. My hair feels light, soft, and I run my fingers through it absentmindedly.

Ashley comes out after a few minutes.

"I&B Heating and Cooling," she says. "I'm sorry, but I had to come right out and ask. They didn't have anything on their uniforms except their names. I was subtle though. I said my cousin wanted to get, like, an apprenticeship in heating and cooling, and they told me he should give Ike a call—he owns the place. I even got a business card." She looks a little worried. "Is that okay?"

I grin, almost as much because she's anxious as because she actually got the job done. "Not bad. You could be a spy or something." I take the business card from her and tuck it in my pocket. This has been quite a day so far. Yesterday at this time I was friendless and depressed; today I have not only a new friend but also an accomplice. This is a new sensation for me: I'm actually having fun.

We stop across the street for a shawarma, which turns out to be sort of a chicken-and-tomato sandwich wrapped in a pita, and then Ashley drives me home. The roads are slick and slushy, and I grip the overhead safety handle, my jaw clenched as I wonder what it will feel like when we skid out and crash into a parked car or the side of a building. Somehow, though, we make it to the parking lot of my building and Ashley lets me out.

I open the door and pause a second before I step out in the snow. "Thanks. I had a good day."

Ashley grins. "Me too. We'll have to ditch again sometime."

"Be careful in this snow. I'd hate for you to crash the car before you even get your license."

* * *

The snow is starting to blow around, whipping at my ears, tangling up my new hairdo and flying down the back of my coat, getting my neck wet. My shoes are soaked by the time I get to the door of my building. I pause just inside the vestibule and pull out my cell phone to check the time. I figure I'll just have time to duck upstairs and stash my new clothes in my room before the kids' bus comes. I'm sure Simon will have something to say about my haircut.If I was a better liar, I'm sure I could make up a fabulous story about how I got paint in my hair in art class and had to run down the street to get an emergency trim or something. As it is, though, I decide my best bet is to be vague.

I open the apartment door, expecting to see Simon crashed out on the couch watching *Oprah* or sitting at the kitchen table doing the sudoku. What I'm not expecting is a living room full of little kids twenty minutes before the bus is supposed to be here, and Simon standing in the hallway with the phone tucked between his shoulder and his ear and the phone book in his hands.

"Never mind," he says, glaring at me. "She's here."

I freeze, my arms full of bags and my new hairdo wet with snow and sticking to my face. "What's going on? It's not even three o'clock. The kids' bus isn't even supposed to be here yet."

"The schools closed at noon because of the storm. Which you'd know, if you'd been *at* school today." Simon looks me up and down. "What did you do, ditch to go shopping? What the hell has gotten into you?"

I shrug. "I just…thought it was time for a change."

Simon shrugs back, mocking me. "Time for a change. Sure, great. Change away. Cut off all your hair. Drop out of school. Why don't you get pregnant and dive into a pile of drugs while you're at it? Turn into Emily. That'd be a nice change."

"What's your problem? I missed one day of school—that's hardly dropping out. And apparently it was only a half day, after all that."

"Is it your new little friend? What's her name, Amber? Was this her idea?"

"Ashley. And no." I can't look right at him when I lie, but who cares whose idea it was? I'm not sorry we did it.

"You left a bunch of little kids standing out at the bus stop in a blizzard. Crying out loud, Jenna, you're supposed to be the responsible one."

I've never seen Simon worked up like this. The veins in his neck are bulging out, and his face is turning red.

"Well, maybe I'm sick of being so frigging responsible." I kick off my boots, throw my coat down on the floor. The kids are all staring at me, but I don't care. I bundle up all my bags and storm down the hall to my room. I try to slam the door, but Emily has hung a shirt over the top, so it bounces back open again and I have to take the shirt off the door before I can really get a good *THUD* out of it. I climb the ladder to my bed and pull the covers over my head. Why did there have to be a stupid snowstorm today?

* * *

One by one the kids leave; I hear their moms asking where I am.

I hear Simon's voice. "She's not feeling well." Nice of him to lie for me, I suppose. At least now I don't look as irresponsible as he thinks I am. As I actually *am*, I suppose.

After a while—half an hour, maybe more; it's hard to tell with my head buried under my pillow—I hear Simon padding down the hall. He's coming to talk to me. Ugh. He knocks, then opens the door after a minute when I don't say anything.

"Hey. You still in here?"

"Where else would I be, you flying jackass?"

He flops down on the bottom bunk, making the whole bed sway a little. "No need to be rude. For what it's worth, it's about time you got your hair cut."

"Gee, thanks."

Simon puts his feet up against the bottom of my bed and gives the chunk of plywood supporting my mattress a kick. "Come on. There's no need to be nasty. I just...it's weird for you not to come home from school on time. And you've never missed meeting the kids' bus before. So when Katie said you weren't even at school today..."

"You talked to Katie?" I sit up abruptly, bumping my head on the stucco ceiling. "Ow. Crap. What'd you call her for?"

"Who else was I going to call? I don't have your new friend's phone number."

"Ashley. Her name is Ashley. And I don't understand what the big deal is about skipping school. It's not like I make a habit of it."

"I certainly hope not. You're the only one in this family who has a chance to make something of themselves.

I'd hate for you to blow it off for a new haircut and a couple pairs of jeans."

"I'm not going to flunk out over one missed day. And I don't know exactly what you expect me to make of myself. It's not like I'm some kind of genius."

"Yeah, I know. I've seen your report cards." He gives the plywood another kick, bumping my head off the ceiling again.

"Ow! Cut it out, you big wiener."

"Look, I'm trying to be serious." He stands up on the bottom bunk so he can lean on the railing and stare me down. I put my hand on his forehead, push him away.

"Well, you suck at it."

"I know. I don't get a lot of practice. But don't you want more out of life than this? You're not much of a scholar, but you've got half a brain if you'd focus."

"Gee, thanks. And what exactly am I supposed to be focusing on?"

"The future. Getting out of this neighborhood. Not getting pregnant when you're sixteen and winding up a crack whore in some dive apartment over a pawnshop on Kenilworth."

"Aw, there go all my hopes and dreams, Simon. You're such a spoilsport."

I lie back on the bed for a few minutes, staring up at the ceiling at pictures of my dad that I found loose in an old envelope and taped up there. Dad behind the counter of his store, Dad setting up the Christmas tree, Momma and Dad on their wedding day, a million years ago in the seventies when collars were wide and big hair was in vogue. Simon makes no move to leave, and just lies there on Emily's bed for a while. I finally figure I should break the silence.

"Do you ever think about Travis Bingham?" I ask.

Simon doesn't say anything for so long that I think maybe he's fallen asleep. "No," he says finally, decisively. "Why would I?"

"I don't know." I wonder how much to tell him. Somehow, after his reaction to my skipping school, I don't think I should tell him I've turned into a stalker. "It's just…think about how different things would have been without him."

There's another long silence before he says anything else. "Things are the way they are, Jenna," is what he finally comes up with. "I don't see much point in worrying about things that aren't. You can't change anything by wasting time on what-ifs." He sighs and gets up. "For what it's worth, your hair looks pretty good."

"Doesn't it?" I roll over, slide down the ladder to the floor. "And wait till you see what I got." I pull out the clothes Ashley picked out for me and lay them out on Emily's bed so he can see them. "Who knew I looked so good in blue?"

Simon cuffs me good-naturedly on the ear. "When did you turn into such a girl, anyway?"

I give him a shove. "Shut up, you giant turd. And get out of my room."

I close the door behind him and grab my knitting, a sweater I'm working on for Simon. I flop down on the chair in the corner, an overstuffed monstrosity so covered in clothes that it's hard to tell what color the fabric is. It's brown corduroy, for the record, a holdover from the seventies, worn thin in spots and patched to the extent of my mom's sewing ability, which was never great. Knitting was always more her thing, although she hasn't done it in years. I guess it's my thing now. It calms me down. Besides, people usually like the stuff I knit for them—or they pretend to, anyway. This sweater for Simon is nice; I got a real bargain on this fluffy wool blend when the yarn store on Ottawa Street went out of business. I was rich at the time, with almost two hundred dollars I'd saved up from babysitting and from feeding old Mrs. Goldfarb's cats while she was down in Florida, and

I blew every penny of it at the yarn store's closing sale. There are still bags in the Rubbermaid containers in my room and a few more in the basement that I haven't even touched yet, but I figured it was worth it. Who knows when they're going to open another yarn store around here where I can get good stuff? I could always go to Walmart, but all they sell there is the crappy acrylic stuff that rubs my hands raw and feels like plastic fishing line against my fingers. I'll use that stuff in a pinch, when I have to knit something I don't care much about—a baby sweater for one of the moms in our building, or a pair of slippers for Momma that's just going to get stolen by one of the other crazies in her home. But when I want to make something nice, something I'm really going to enjoy making, I'll dip into my stash of the good stuff.

Still, I don't feel much like doing anything nice for Simon right now. Not after he went and got all…parental… like that. I tuck the sweater back in the Rubbermaid container with the sticky note on the side that says *Work In Progress* and pull out a fresh ball of yarn. It's bright green, made of cotton, and I run it through my fingers for a few minutes, trying to decide what to make of it. It's going to have to be a small project; I only have a couple of balls of this stuff, and it's too rough to be a baby sweater. I think about Mr. Morrison, the old man who lives upstairs with his little dog, Buster. I twist it around my fingers. Yes, I think Buster would look very smart in this color.

A few minutes online turns up a pattern that will work nicely, a handsome little jacket with buttons up the side and a turtleneck collar. I do a little math; if I want to make the sweater the same size as the pattern, I'll need a set of number nine needles. I look through my boxes but don't find any. Damn it.

I run through a quick inventory in my head of the assorted craft supplies packed in boxes in the basement. There may be a set downstairs. So much for holing up in my room for the evening.

"Simon, I need your keys to the storage locker."

"All right. You know where to find them."

He doesn't ask what I need; he rarely does. Usually I don't even ask him for the keys—I just take them—but after the blowout we had earlier, I figure I'd rather avoid any chance of conflict for the rest of the night.

I put on my slippers—that concrete floor downstairs gets cold—and head down the hall to the stairs. A couple of the older kids from upstairs are going outside to throw snowballs in the parking lot, all bundled up in their coats and mittens. For a second I think back to last winter, when Griffin and Marie-Claire and Katie and

I all had a huge romp through Gage Park in a blizzard, throwing snowballs and rolling around and making a snowman as tall as Griffin until we were all soaked and laughing hysterically. Suddenly I miss them, and I feel my eyes burn a little as I tear up. But I blink away the tears and shake my head. I guess I'm too old for that stuff anyway. I had a great time with Ashley, but I can't picture her doing any of those things. I can't imagine the cool kids ever getting goofy like that.

Down in the basement, I step over the boxes that contain Simon's yearbooks and the newspaper clippings I was showing Ashley the other day. Emily banished three or four boxes of my surplus craft supplies down here last year, because she kept tripping over them on her way to bed in the middle of the night. Somehow they'd got shuffled to the back of the locker when Simon pulled out the Christmas tree, a box of old clothes, whatever. I move boxes aside, building a wall between me and the open door of the locker that makes me a little nervous. It's a bit creepy down here at the best of times, and when I look back at the tower of boxes behind me, I let out a little shudder. I've seen rats down here. There's no quick way of getting out of here if one suddenly crawls out from between a pile of boxes.

I shove aside open boxes, stacks of old photo albums and a milk crate full of baby toys until I finally get to the big Rubbermaid containers of yarn in the back of the locker. There's a huge bouquet of knitting needles in there: round needles, bamboo needles, plastic and metal needles in just about every size. I find a couple of mismatched number nines, but by now I can't stop thinking about rats and cockroaches and spiders and whatever other manner of wildlife might be down here. I tuck the needles into the back pocket of my new jeans and start restacking the boxes. It takes me a few minutes to get everything rearranged again. It's like playing Tetris in real life. I don't know why I'm suddenly so creeped out being in the basement by myself; I've been down here dozens of times on my own. But suddenly I'm noticing the *thunk, thunk, thunk* of the boiler, the rattling of the overhead pipes as someone upstairs turns on their shower, the sound of someone pushing an old wheeled cart down the hall to the laundry room. I get everything stacked back up and am about to hightail it out of the locker room when my arm brushes a pile of boxes, and the whole thing crashes to the floor.

"Crap," I say out loud, startled at the sound of my own voice. Some of the boxes have spewed out their contents in the avalanche, and with a sigh I squat down to start repacking them. One of the dumped boxes has all of Simon's old papers in it, the one I've been through so many times I don't even need to look at the newspaper clippings one by one to tell you what they say. I find the green file folder they belong in and start to tuck the papers back into it, calming down a little as I see the familiar words and pictures on the familiar yellowed bits of paper. This part I've done before. And with the open door behind me, I can outrun a rat or a spider if the need arises. I find myself lingering a little over the old stories, smoothing them out, tucking them back in like old friends. My life was much simpler, I think, when these were my only connection to Travis Bingham. Before I was stalking him. Maybe Katie and Simon are right: maybe I should just give up on looking for answers and get on with my life.

I pick up the stack of yearbooks that's fallen out of the box with the newspaper clippings and slide them one by one back into the box. For some reason I linger over the last book, the one Ashley and I were looking at. I idly flip through the back pages to see if I can find any other pictures of Simon. There are a few besides his basketball picture and goofy-looking headshot. True enough, he wasn't a bad-looking guy back in high school. There are pictures of him surrounded by girls in the cafeteria, looking preppy and popular, exactly like the kind of kid who's tormented me and my friends since kindergarten. I wonder what he'd have thought back then if he'd known he'd end up the superintendent of a slum apartment building instead of some college football superstar or something.

I'm about to close the book when an inscription on the inside of the back cover catches my eye. Written in red marker, in a tidy but definitely masculine hand, it says *To the best friend a guy could hope to have. See you lots this summer, Travis.*

I can feel something happening to my stomach, like it's doing backflips. Could it be? How common a name could Travis be? I've never known anyone else by that name, but maybe fifteen years ago it was as trendy as Josh or Madison.

I look again at the photos of Simon. There are no pictures of him with Travis Bingham. But underneath each and every candid picture of my brother, printed in tiny italics, is the same thing: *T. Bingham, photo.*

I perch on a pile of boxes for a long time, fretting, festering, fidgeting. I take the knitting needles out of my back pocket and twirl them in my hands like drumsticks. I use the metal tip of one to poke a hole in the corner of one of the cardboard boxes, digging at it until the entire corner is ruined. So this is why Simon never wants to talk about Travis Bingham. I wonder how long before my dad's murder they stopped being friends. Travis would have signed Simon's yearbook in June. My dad died in October. Four months. Well, I guess I went from having friends to not having friends in less than twenty-four hours. Maybe four months is a reasonable amount of time to go from best friend to murderer.

Suddenly I remember something my mother said when I saw her on Sunday, after I told her I'd seen Travis. *Such a nice boy,* she'd said. I'd thought she was just off on one of her nonsensical rants, but if Travis and Simon were friends, she might have actually known what she was talking about for once.

I contemplate taking a bus up the Mountain to talk to her, but in this weather the buses probably aren't even running. I don't feel much like going back upstairs. I wonder whether anyone would notice if I just stayed down here overnight. In the good old days—like, last week—if I was pissed off at Simon, I would just go sleep over at Katie's house, but that clearly isn't an option right now. I'm not ready to ask Simon about Travis Bingham yet—what would I even say? But I can't stay down here forever. It's cold and clammy and thoughts of rats and roaches are starting to cross my mind again, so eventually I bite the bullet, lock up the storage room and head upstairs.

Simon and Wex are eating pizza in front of the TV. I toss Simon his keys and grab a piece of pizza to take to my room with me.

"You were down there long enough, I was ready to send out a search party."

"Yeah, well, some boxes fell over. I had to pick them up."

"Okay. So, are you just going to be cranky and snippy for the entire rest of the night, or should I be prepared to enjoy this treatment for the rest of the week?"

"I haven't decided yet."

There's nothing hanging on the top of my door, so the sound when I slam it this time is much more satisfying. I turn the computer screen so I can see the knitting pattern from my chair in the corner and set to work casting on stitches. Soon I'm lost in the rhythmic clicking of the needles, the feel of the wool between my fingers. I don't know where to put this new information in my head: that my brother, the only constant and reliable person in my entire stinking life, was apparently best friends with the man who killed my father.

WEDNESDAY

I wake up to Simon knocking on my door. "You gonna sleep all day?"

"Hmm?"

"It's nine thirty. Are you planning to get up at some point?"

I look at the clock and panic. Did I forget to set my alarm? I must have. It's my own fault; I was up late, stewing and knitting. On the bright side, I'm nearly done the doggy sweater. But I'm sure missing school entirely one day and then being late the next is going to set Simon off on another lecture session. I roll out of bed and hop down the ladder to the floor. "Can you drive me to school? I don't know what happened to my alarm."

"I can drive you, but there's not going to be anybody there. It's a snow day."

I blink, wondering if I'm missing something. "Then why are you waking me up if I don't have to go to school?"

He shrugs. "I don't know, you don't usually sleep in this late. I just thought I'd check and make sure everything was all right."

Forgetting for a second that I'm already mad at him, I get mad all over again. "That's the most ridiculous thing I've ever heard. Could you *be* a bigger jerk? Seriously."

"Well, excuse me for being concerned."

"You don't need to be. I can take care of myself."

He lets out a weird little sigh. "Yeah, I know you can."

I open the curtains, have a look out at the street. It's still snowing, but nothing like what it was yesterday. The snowplows are out, and the blue-and-yellow-on-white HSR buses are slogging their way through the slush.

I shove Simon out of the way to get to my dresser, where I grab one of my new shirts and a pair of jeans. "I'm going to shower, and then I'm going out for a while."

"Where to? None of the stores are going to be open, and I thought all your cronies weren't speaking to you."

"I'm going to see Momma."

He lets out a barking laugh that sounds like a wounded seal. "You're kidding, right?"

"Why would I be kidding?"

"Because every time we go there, I practically—and sometimes literally, come to think of it—have to drag you there kicking and screaming."

"Well, today I want to go."

Simon looks baffled, but he doesn't ask for an explanation. "Do you, um, want me to drive you?"

"No thanks. I'll take the bus."

* * *

As soon as I get outside, I almost regret not accepting a ride, although having Simon along on this trip would be most inappropriate. The snow is up to my knees in the parking lot, and my old sneakers certainly aren't built for this weather. There's usually a bus along this route every ten minutes or so, but with the snow I guess they're running behind, so my feet are soaked by the time one finally comes. I sit with my feet against the heater, willing my shoes to dry. I'm not one for superstition, but I spend most of the bus ride with my fingers crossed, hoping against hope that, first of all, Momma is having one of her more lucid days and is not a raving lunatic, and second, that the bus doesn't spin out and career all the way down the Mountain, killing everyone on board.

By the time I get up the hill, it's almost noon, I've been on three different buses, and I'm soaked to the knee. I sign in at the visitors' desk, then duck into the public bathroom and take off my jeans and socks to wave them under the air dryer. It takes awhile to get my clothes to the point where I'm willing to put them back on again, and I use the time to think about how best to approach Momma. She's not much on answering direct questions, so getting information out of her is tricky at the best of times.

Momma is having lunch when I finally get to her room: tuna salad on whole-wheat bread and a bowl of chicken noodle soup. Most of the residents eat in the dining room, but Momma isn't much for mixing. She throws such a fit whenever they take her out of her room that I guess they finally just decided to bring her meals to her. She's out of bed, though, which is unusual, and sitting at a little table in the corner.

"Hey, Momma." I perch on the edge of her bed. "That soup looks pretty good."

"Oh, hello." She looks up at me, her eyes wide and unblinking, and I know she has no clue who I am. "It is very nice soup. Would you like some of it?"

"No thanks."

"All right."

She's not doing too well with the spoon, dribbling soup all over the place, and finally I figure I should give her a hand. "Here. Let me do that." I spoon the rest of the bowl into her, then break her sandwich up into quarters and hand her a piece.

"I'm sorry, I don't remember your name," Momma says.

"It's Jenna."

"Oh, that's a lovely name. I have a little girl named Jenna."

Ordinarily I'd kick up a fuss at this, maybe yell at her. I don't get why she knows who Simon is—and sometimes Emily—but never recognizes me or Wex. But this time I bite my lip, figuring diplomacy is the order of the day. "I know," I tell her. I brace myself for a second, then figure it's best to dive right in. "Hey, do you remember Travis Bingham?"

"Oh, yes. Travis. A lovely boy. So handsome. He has the kindest eyes. A beautiful bright green. Almost yellow, like a cat's. Very unusual. He's Simon's friend."

The knot in my stomach tightens. Up to this point, there has still been a chance that this is all a mistake on my part—it was some other Travis who signed Simon's yearbook, some other T. Bingham who took all those pictures. But Momma seems pretty sure of herself.

I shift my weight, steeling myself for whatever comes next. "Tell me more about Travis."

"Oh, such a terrible family he came from. So much fighting, and his father drunk all the time. That's why we invited him to come and live with us."

I blink. There's no way I heard that right. "I'm sorry, what?"

"It was only supposed to be for a few days at first, but I suppose all told it wound up being close to six months."

"Travis Bingham *lived* with us?" I think that over for a second and realize it's not entirely accurate. This would have been before I was born. "I mean, with you?"

Momma gives me this weird blink, like her internal computer has gone into screen-saver mode. "I'm sorry, dear. I didn't catch your name."

And that's all I get from her. I ask her half a dozen other questions, but she suddenly goes off on a rant about how the family in the next room is trying to kill her, which of course is ridiculous because there's obviously not a family living next door to her. In fact, the guy who lives in the room next to her is a quadriplegic who can't even wipe his own butt, let alone carry out a murder plot. After ten or fifteen minutes of this nonsense, I tell Momma I have to go.

Momma grabs my hand as I stand up to go, and for a second I think she might be about to give me one last tidbit of information—like why Travis was so angry at my dad that he resorted to murder—but I have no such luck.

"Nurse," she says. "Can you tell the housekeepers not to put the blue sheets on my bed anymore? The green sheets are much softer."

I pat her on the hand. "Sure. I'll let them know."

* * *

I stew over what Momma has told me all the way home. It's not like Travis killing my dad has ever been a secret: I remember Momma telling me the story way back when I was in kindergarten. We had a substitute teacher the day we were making Father's Day cards, who seemed annoyed when half the kids in the class told her they didn't have dads.

"You must have one," she told us. "He might not live in your house, but everybody's got a father somewhere. Maybe you can mail it to him."

So I made my card and brought it home to Momma, and asked when we could go see my dad to deliver it. That's when she first pulled out the green folder with all the newspaper clippings to show me what had happened.

"Your daddy was a great man," she told me. "But sometimes there are bad people in the world, and it was a very bad man named Travis Bingham who took your daddy away from us."

*　*　*

I lean back against the bus window, feeling the condensation on the glass making my hair damp and clammy. So now Momma's telling me Travis Bingham wasn't such a bad man after all. At least, not when she invited him to live with them. I wonder what could have gone so wrong that he'd want to kill my father.

If only there was someone I could ask, someone who was there at the time. Simon's made it pretty clear that he's not interested in talking about any of this, and Emily—

"Emily." Once again I find myself speaking out loud on the bus. Emily was ten when my dad died. If Travis lived with my family when he was in high school, she would have been five or six at least. She probably remembers part of it. I wonder if I can get her to make any more sense than Momma did.

Simon's vacuuming the hall outside our apartment when I get in, and I dodge him before he can say anything. He'll be another hour, at least, vacuuming all the hallway

WHATEVER DOESN'T KILL YOU

carpets and then washing the tile floors. Not that it'll make much difference. You can clean it up all you want, but this place will always be a hole.

For once I'm actually hoping to find Emily crashed out on the couch or her bunk, but of course I have no such luck. Wex is plunked in front of the TV as usual, blasting away at spaceships on his PlayStation.

I head to my room, where I kick off my soggy sneakers and put them against the baseboard heater to dry, then peel off my socks and replace them with a pair of fuzzy knitted slippers. I'm about to flop down in the corner chair to knit when it occurs to me: Wex might know where Emily is. I haven't seen her in a couple of days, which usually means either she's got a new boyfriend somewhere or she's in jail or the hospital. None of those things would be a surprise.

"Hey, dude." I perch on the couch beside him. "Whatcha playing?"

"*Colony Wars*." He looks at me suspiciously. "Why do you want to know? You're not watching TV right now, Uncle Simon said I could play PlayStation."

"That's fine. I don't want to watch TV. I just wanted to know if you've talked to your mom in the last couple of days."

He thinks that over carefully for a minute, gnawing at his lower lip with that one giant adult tooth of his.

Maybe the poor kid will be less goofy-looking when his other baby teeth fall out, but I doubt it. "I think she was here yesterday for a little while. She said she got a new job, and then she left again."

"A job?" That sounds shady to me—probably illegal.

"Yeah. Aw, damn it, you made me die." He throws his controller down and scowls at me.

"Sorry. And watch your language. What kind of job?"

Wex sighs, clearly disappointed that he didn't get a bigger rise out of me, and picks up his controller again. "Washing dishes at Mr. Woo's."

"Hmm. That's not bad."

Wex shrugs. "She says it sucks ass."

"Dude. Language."

"Whatever."

I cuff him lightly across the back of the head. Strange: he's not usually this disagreeable. "Where did this attitude come from all of a sudden?"

"I'm mad 'cause you were fighting with Uncle Simon. How come you're being such a bitch to him all of a sudden?"

"Because..." I weigh the idea of telling him what I've found out about Simon and Travis Bingham. But he's way too young to understand, and all this stuff is ancient history to him. "Because he can be a huge weenie sometimes."

"Yeah, I guess."

"And don't say *bitch*. It's not nice."

Mr. Woo's. I've never eaten there myself—rumor has it they use cat meat in the chicken balls—but at least it sounds like an actual, honest-to-gosh job. I stand up, debating putting on my sodden sneakers and wading back out in the storm, but one look at the snow whirling around the parking lot and the cars skidding and skittering along the road makes me decide that perhaps Jenna Cooper, Girl Detective is going to sit this one out. After all, I've waited fifteen years for answers. Another day isn't going to kill me, but another trip out in that blizzard might.

THURSDAY

The snow has stopped by the time I wake up and stumble out to the kitchen, where I'm disappointed to find Wex sitting at the table, all ready for school.

"You should really get dressed," he says through a mouthful of something neon-colored with marshmallows. "It's not a snow day today."

"Damn it."

"Language." He swallows his mouthful of Day-Glo cereal and sticks out his tongue at me, brightly colored crumbs still stuck all over it.

"Ew. Disgusting." I head off to the shower. I'm not used to having so little hair, and I use way too much shampoo.

By the time I get it all rinsed out and decide which of my new clothes to wear—I pick an emerald-green T-shirt, with a grey hoodie over it, and a pair of jeans that Ashley said make my butt look great—I'm running late, and I really have to hustle to make it to school on time.

I'm still earlier than Marie-Claire, though, and I can't help but notice the double take she does when she sees me. She gives me this awkward little smile when she spies me looking at her, then quickly looks away and makes a point of sitting at a table on the other side of the room from me. All through class, though, I catch her looking in my direction, checking out my new haircut and new clothes. I can't tell if she's jealous or judgmental or both, but I guess it doesn't matter one way or another. It's not like we're friends anymore.

I look for Ashley in the hall between classes, hoping for a friendly face, but all I get are Marie-Claire and Katie chatting away with their backs to me when I go to my locker. It seemed like a great idea back in September, all of us getting our lockers so close together, but now it's just awkward.

"Do you want to come over tonight?"

I look up, wondering if Katie's talking to me all of a sudden, but of course not—she's asking Marie-Claire.

"Ah, I can't. I'm going to a party. At the university, you know? I'd invite you along, but *alors*, you don't have a fake ID."

Katie lets out a little sigh that sounds like she's trying not to let her disappointment show. "That's okay. Another time."

In gym class Ashley comes burbling over to me, chattering away about how great my hair still looks. I didn't get any new clothes I could wear in gym, so I'm still stuck in my ratty old track pants and one of Simon's T-shirts that comes almost to my knees. It's volleyball today, which I'm sure suits Katie fine, since it doesn't require partners and all she really has to do is step out of the way when the ball comes anywhere near her. But Ashley and I wind up on one team and Katie is on the other, so the whole time we're standing together and Ashley is talking to me, I can see Katie staring daggers at us through the net. I can't help but feel bad for her, especially having heard Marie-Claire brush her off not half an hour ago, but at the same time, she is the one who engineered all my other friends dumping me.

Ashley slides up to me in the changeroom afterward, oblivious to the fact that both Katie and all of Ashley's former friends are staring.

"So, what did your brother say about your hair?"

"He said it looked good. After he busted me for skipping school."

"Oh, crappy. For what it's worth, my dad almost nailed me for taking the car. He didn't think there was enough snow on it for it to have been sitting there all day."

"Oh no! What did you tell him?"

"I said I left my school bag in the backseat and had to go get it because my homework was in it, and I thought I would brush off the car to be nice." She rolls her eyes. "He's so gullible. All I have to do is act like a total ditz and he'll believe anything I tell him."

I think back to her performance with Travis at the hair salon, and I wonder how much of Ashley's day-to-day existence is an act...including her sudden friendship with me.

"Well...I'm glad you didn't get in trouble."

"Even if I did, he always gets over it pretty fast. So what did you do yesterday?"

"I went to see my mom."

"Wow, in the insane asylum?"

"Um, it's a nursing home, but yeah." I watch Katie tuck her regular clothes under her arm and duck into a toilet stall to change. I can tell from the look on her face that she's trying not to cry. I look back at Ashley, determined not to let it get to me. Katie brought this on herself, after all. "So what are you doing tonight?"

"I don't know. You want to do something?" Ashley pulls a pack of gum—the kind with the liquid center—out of her purse and pops a piece into her mouth. "Gum?"

I take a piece—I never turn down an offer of gum or breath mints, because you never know when it's a hint. I give Ashley a good once-over. If I'm thinking about tracking down my sister and getting her take on the Travis Bingham situation, and if I'm playing detective, I could do a lot worse for a sidekick than someone as quick on her feet as Ashley. "I was thinking of going for some Chinese food," I tell her. "You want to come along?"

* * *

After school I find Simon up on the third floor, cleaning out 318. The potheads who lived there were two months behind on their rent and bailed when they found the eviction notice on their door. "Hey," I say. "I need twenty bucks."

He looks up from scrubbing a nasty brown smear off the wall of the living room. He's wearing a paper mask and rubber gloves, and sweating so much that his hair is slicked down over his forehead.

"What is that?" I ask him.

"Three guesses. Bunch of idiots."

"They smeared...poop on the wall?" I can feel my face squinching up in disgust. "That's so nasty."

"I need a can of gasoline and a match for this apartment. Burn it out and start from scratch." The mask wiggles up and down as he talks. If it weren't so disgusting in here, I would laugh at him.

The mess really is incredible. There's a hole through the bathroom door like someone has punched it, a huge stain on the floor that may or may not be blood and, of course, the poop on the walls. I guess they really wanted to send Simon a message of some kind, although I can't imagine why. It's not like he had much choice about kicking them out—not when they weren't paying their rent. And it's not like Simon owns the building—he just collects the rent and plunges the toilets. And scrapes caca off the walls. It literally is a crappy job. For a second I feel sorry for him, but then I remember why I'm here.

"So, twenty bucks."

"Don't you have a job or something? Oh, wait. You blew all your money on a haircut and new clothes, so now you need a loan."

"Um, a loan?"

He laughs. "Of course. Not a loan: a gift. And what do I get out of this?"

Not much point in lying at this point, I may as well tell him where the money's going. "Uh, I'm going out for Chinese food with Ashley. I'll bring you back some leftovers."

"Chinese, huh?" He uses the back of his wrist to push the mask down off his mouth. "What restaurant?"

"I think she said Mr. Woo's." I watch his face carefully for a reaction, but there isn't one; I guess he doesn't know Emily is working there. If she even is. It wouldn't be the first time she's lied to Wex.

"All right." He peels off one glove, fishes his wallet out of the back pocket of his jeans and hands it to me. "Take what you need. Bring me back a combo four."

"What's in a combo four?"

"I don't know. I've never eaten at Mr. Woo's. But combo four is always the best choice."

* * *

Combo four, it turns out, is chicken balls with spareribs, fried rice and mixed vegetables. The egg roll is a dollar extra, but I figure since dinner is on Simon anyway, I'll splurge. I opt for combo two myself—chicken with mushrooms, sweet-and-sour pork and those skinny noodles on the side. I've never been inside Mr. Woo's before, but it's cleaner than you'd think from the dingy, coal-flecked exterior. It's a long, skinny room with black-and-gold wallpaper, a red carpet and little fake candles on the tables. There's a two-foot-high bronze Buddha on the takeout counter by the front door. Our waiter's name is Dave, which disappoints me a little. It's embossed on a little silver name tag that looks like it's been through the laundry with his shirt a few times. He's Asian but doesn't have an accent, which somehow makes the whole place seem less exotic to me. Mr. Woo's is about as close as I'm ever going to get to China. The least Dave could do is make the experience more authentic for me.

Still, it's a little odd being at a sit-down restaurant where they bring the food to your table. Other than when Katie's mom takes us out for dinner, I think the last time I actually had a waiter and a menu was back when Momma was more or less holding things together, working at the No Frills as a cashier, and we used to go to Swiss Chalet on Thursday nights after she got paid.

Ashley is obviously used to eating in restaurants and even manages the chopsticks like she knows what she's doing. Once we get our meals—including Simon's in a Styrofoam takeout container—Ashley leans across the table with a conspiratorial grin. I've told her why we're here, and I think she's excited to have another project. As detective's sidekicks go, she's kind of a natural.

"So, what's the big plan?"

"I don't know…ask Dave the waiter if Emily's working and find out if she has a break coming up?"

"Oh." She looks disappointed, like she was expecting something more dramatic. "Yeah, I guess that'll work."

When Dave brings the bill, I lean back in my chair a little, like I couldn't care less about the answer, and ask him if Emily Cooper is working tonight.

"Oh, Emily? Yeah, I think she just went out back to have a smoke. You want me to tell her you said hi?"

"No, that's fine." I hold back a grin and leave Dave the twenty Simon gave me, which isn't much of a tip on a seventeen-dollar tab, but it's all I have so it'll have to do. The alley that leads to the back of the building is two stores over, so I have to hustle a little to make it there before she finishes her cigarette. I'm still wriggling into my coat as I round the corner into the back alley.

Sure enough, Emily is leaning on the Dumpster, sucking on a cigarette, her holey, faded parka pulled on over her dingy kitchen whites.

"So this is where you've been hiding out these days."

She looks startled to see me but not unduly annoyed. "This isn't where your gang usually hangs out, is it?"

I shrug. "I guess I've got a new gang now."

Emily looks suspicious. "What happened to the old gang?"

Another shrug. I'm not really sure how to answer that. "You know. People grow in different directions."

"That's a load of horse crap."

"Okay. So apparently I did something to piss one of them off and now none of them are talking to me. So I'm branching out. Making new friends. You know."

"Well. Sometimes it's good to get rid of your old friends." Emily takes another drag on her cigarette, looking philosophical. With her hair all tucked back in a hairnet, she looks older than usual, and the security lighting in the back alley makes long, thin shadows of the lines starting to develop around her eyes. Suddenly I'm sorry for her, a little. It's bad enough that I lost a father I never got the chance to know; Emily actually lost her daddy. No wonder she's so screwed up.

"Are you getting rid of your old friends too?" I ask.

"I guess so. Trying to put my life in some kind of order, you know?"

"That's great. I hope it works this time."

"Gee, thanks." She doesn't say it sarcastically, though, so she must know what I mean. She's tried getting her act together more than once, but it would be great for Wex if it finally worked. And for her, too, I suppose. She spends so much time being horrible that it's easy to forget there's a person in there.

"So, um…I didn't just happen to be in the neighborhood, you know."

"No?"

"No. I, um, wanted to ask you something. About Travis Bingham."

"Oh, for crying out loud. Jenna, would you let it go already? That was forever ago. He's nobody. He's a ghost. He's sitting in prison somewhere, and he's probably going to die there."

"He's out. I've met him."

Emily pauses with the cigarette halfway to her lips. "What?"

"He's out on parole, working for some heating company. He came in to fix the heater at the salon where I got my hair cut." I decide to leave out the part where I stalked him at his halfway house. In hindsight, that part's probably more than a little creepy.

"How did you know—"

"I've seen his picture a million times, Em. And I talked to Momma; I know he used to live with us."

Emily narrows her eyes at me, and I recognize the way she tips her head just slightly to one side as a sure sign she's about to let me have it. "With *us*? No, not with *you*. Dad kicked him out when *you* were born. Said he was done feeding other people's kids."

Of all the reactions I could have gotten from Emily at the mention of Travis's name, this is the last one I would have expected. There's no anger at the idea of Dad's death. She's not worried about Travis roaming the streets. Instead, she seems to be mad at *me*, not for anything I've done, but just for being born and getting Travis kicked out of our house. I take a step back from Emily, stumbling into a dingy snowbank, and soaking my leg to the knee for the second time in as many days.

"So Dad kicked Travis out...and Travis killed him?"

Emily shrugs, takes one last drag on her cigarette, then flicks the butt almost but not quite at me. It lands on the shoveled path in front of me. "I guess so. Look, what difference does it make? Dad's dead, Travis did his time. Life goes on, right?"

"I...yeah. I guess so." I still have more questions than answers, but it looks like Emily has reached the end of her patience with me. I step out of the snowbank and shake the dirty snow off my pants as well as I can. "Thanks."

Emily looks surprised. "Sure. Don't worry about it." She grinds out the still-glowing cigarette butt with the toe of one of her Doc Marten's as I turn to go. "Hey, Jenna."

"Yeah?"

There's a funny look on her face when I look back at her, like she's thinking real hard about something. "How did he look when you saw him? Travis, I mean. Did he look...okay?"

"I guess so. What do you mean?"

"Did he look happy? Or...healthy? Or...I don't know. Do you think he's doing okay?"

How do I answer that? He looked like an older version of the man who destroyed my family—only somehow I know that's the wrong thing to say to Emily right now.

"He looked fine," I tell her instead. "Yeah. He looked good."

* * *

So now I know why Travis shot my dad, anyway. Score another one for Jenna Cooper, Girl Detective. If his life at home was as horrible as Momma told me, I can see why he'd have been mad. But if he was such a nice guy, like she'd also said, why wouldn't he have been able to come up with another place to stay instead of resorting to violence?

I come back around the corner of the alley, deep in thought, and run full-on into Ashley. Our heads crack together and we both let out a yell. Funny—in the time I've been talking to Emily, Ashley has almost slipped my mind. I give her a halfhearted smack on the shoulder.

"You scared the crap out of me. Where were you, anyway?"

"I was trying to pay my bill. I had so much junk in my purse that I couldn't find my debit card, and then when I finally found it, I didn't have enough money in that account and I had to use the emergency ten dollars I keep in the secret pocket in my wallet. Then when I got out of the restaurant, I couldn't find you. And by the time I figured out how to get out to the back alley, it looked like you were really deep in conversation and I didn't want to interrupt."

"Oh." That was considerate of her, I suppose. "Thanks."

"So did your sister tell you anything important?"

"I guess. It was weird. She was more reasonable than she usually is. She wanted to know how Travis is doing."

"Why would she care?"

"I know, right? But when I told her I'd met him, she got all funny. Like…" I search for the word a minute before it finally occurs to me. "Jealous."

"That's so weird. Do you think maybe she was in love with him or something?"

"Dude, she was, like, eight when Travis killed my dad. Maybe she had a crush on him, but she's probably over it by now."

Ashley laughs. "Dude, did you just call me dude?"

That strikes both of us as funny and sets us to laughing so hard we actually get a dirty look from an old guy shoveling his sidewalk. We turn a corner and head off down Barton, cackling like a pair of drunken hyenas.

When we get to the corner of Dunsmure and Ottawa, we go our separate ways. It's getting cold again, and the wet leg of my jeans is starting to freeze in the wind. I pass the Tim Hortons—the original one, a little brick building built way back in the sixties before there was a Tim's on every corner. This one doesn't have a drive-thru, or even much of a parking lot to speak of, so people perch their cars every which way on the little ring of asphalt that surrounds it. There are a few scruffy-looking regulars at the table by the big window, sharing a *Toronto Sun* and a box of Timbits, and a homeless guy smoking a cigarette outside by the door with an empty brown-paper cup in his hand, trolling for change.

It occurs to me that I could use a hot chocolate, and I sift through the change in my pocket to see if I have enough. A dollar sixty-three; plenty for a medium-sized hot chocolate, with a few cents left over to throw in the homeless guy's cup on the way out.

I'm about to step inside when something—or rather, someone—catches my eye. It's Marie-Claire, sitting alone at the little table behind the display case of sports memorabilia and pictures of Tim Horton in his hockey uniform. Marie-Claire is nursing a brown-paper cup of coffee and flipping through a book of crossword puzzles, a pen tucked between two fingers. I stop for a second, my hand on the door, debating whether I should go in. I think of Marie-Claire at school today, telling Katie she couldn't hang out tonight because there was a vampire party at the university. Why on earth would she be doing crossword puzzles in Tim Hortons at nine thirty at night if she was supposed to be at a party all the way across town? Did she make it up so she didn't have to go to Katie's house? Has she been making up the parties and guys all along?

I'm still standing with my hand on the door when a guy with a shaved head and a beer gut so big it almost turns the corner ahead of him brushes past me.

"'Scuse me, sweetheart. You're gettin' between a man and his coffee here."

"Sorry about that."

I back away from the door and drop my buck sixty-three into the homeless guy's coffee cup. I've had enough probing into other people's deep, dark secrets for one night. I'll leave Marie-Claire to hers for the time being.

FRIDAY

Emily is home when my alarm goes off, sleeping soundly and seemingly unmoved by the blaring Middle Eastern music coming out of the clock radio. She's snoring, but quietly for a change. I didn't hear her come in, which is also unusual. Maybe she really is serious about getting her life together; she seems to have come home sober. I watch her sleep for a minute, her eyes lightly closed. She has changed out of her grimy dishwashing uniform into a faded blue nightshirt with Snoopy dressed as Joe Cool on the front. She lets out a little grunt and rolls over, her long, shaggy hair falling across her face. Maybe I should recommend my hairdresser to her.

I jump a little as she sits up suddenly. "Jenna, stop staring at me while I'm trying to sleep."

"Sorry, I was just…" What? Trying to figure out if she's stoned? That isn't a conversation I want to have right now. "…getting ready for school."

"Fine. Get ready and go then. We had a bunch of drunk idiots come in right at closing time and order half the menu. I didn't get home until three fifteen. Let me sleep in, would you?"

Wow. Drunk idiots. Talk about the pot calling the kettle black. But I've had more sensible conversations with my sister in the past twenty-four hours than I have in the past six or seven years, which has got to count for something.

* * *

There's a stiff breeze blowing as I make the trip to school, and I dig my hands into the pockets of Simon's old coat, shivering as I go. I'm half a block away when I see Marie-Claire ahead of me, hunched up in her thin black trench coat, her shoulders around her ears. I'm tempted to ignore her the same way she's been ignoring me all week, but at the same time I'm madly curious about what was going on last night.

"Hey, Marie-Claire. Wait up."

She slows and looks behind her. She doesn't stop when she sees me, but she doesn't speed up either, so I jog a little to catch up. "Long time no see."

She looks a little perplexed. "I saw you yesterday at school."

"Well, true. But I haven't talked to you in awhile. How is everything?"

Marie-Claire shrugs. "It's the same as it always is."

"Been to any good parties lately?" I watch her face carefully, but it doesn't give anything away. I wonder what's going through her head. Did she notice me at the locker yesterday when she was talking to Katie?

"Yeah, a couple. You know me—always out someplace."

"Yep. I know you." At least, I thought I did.

* * *

When I get home after school, the usual crowd of moms is standing at the bus stop, yammering away on their cell phones and puffing on their cigarettes. As I approach, I can see that the cluster looks bigger than usual, with Xavier's mom and the twins' mother waiting to pick up their respective offspring, which means I'm just going to have Wex and Henry today. But wait…I squint, incredulous as I get closer and realize that there, tucked in among the other mothers, is my sister, smoking and chatting away like she's suddenly part of this odd little family.

"You're picking Wex up at the bus?"

Emily looks surprised to see me, despite the fact that I've been the one out here every school day for the past two and a half years, ever since Wex started junior kindergarten. "Yeah, why not? I'm his mother."

Of course I can't think of a single reason why she shouldn't be out here, but I still feel a little put out, like she's stealing my job or something. It doesn't help that when the bus pulls up, Wex bounds off it with a squeal and throws his arms around Emily's legs.

"Mom! You came to meet me!"

She gives him a grin that looks surprisingly...I don't know...human, and hugs him back. "Yep. You want to go out for supper? Momma got paid. We can go to McDonald's if you want; you can play in the PlayPlace."

Wex looks enraptured, even happier than he looked on Christmas morning. I watch the two of them cavorting across the parking lot like old buddies and feel a little sick to my stomach. For all the razzing I've given Emily about being a horrible mother and bugging her to pay more attention to Wex, there's always been a part of me that enjoyed being the one he comes to when he skins his knee or gets teased at school. It hardly seems fair that Emily can just wake up one morning and decide she wants to be a good parent, and suddenly she's his favorite person. It makes me realize what Travis must have felt when I suddenly came along and got him kicked out of his home. For the second time in a week, I've been displaced.

"All right, kiddo." I take Henry by the hand. "I guess it's just you and me today." Henry grins and chatters away as we walk back to the apartment to wait for his mother while Wex and Emily head off to catch the bus to McDonald's. I watch the two of them, hand in hand, feeling somehow empty. Since I lost one mitten at Griffin's on Sunday night, I've made do with cold hands, and I bury the hand that's not holding Henry's in the pocket of my jeans. There's something in there, wrinkled and made of thin cardboard. I pull it out to take a look at it. *I&B HEATING AND COOLING*. The business card of the company where Travis is working. I'm not much on superstition, but I can't help but wonder if this is some kind of sign. I flip the card over and over, weaving it in and out of my fingers as we walk down the hall to the apartment. There's a weird feeling in the pit of my stomach, and I have a sudden urge to drop Henry's hand, turn and run. Travis Bingham is getting his life together: he's out of prison; he's got a job. It hardly seems fair that while he's starting to pull things together, my life is falling apart. In the week since I first saw him staring back at me from that newspaper article, I've lost all my friends, Simon is pissed off at me—or was, at any rate, although I'm still a little sore about that—and now I'm losing Wex too.

Suddenly I'm hoping Henry's mom comes early today; I think the time has come for me to go talk to Travis Bingham.

* * *

I spend the next hour pacing the apartment, ducking into my bedroom and Googling directions and bus routes to I&B Heating and Cooling, then back out to the living room to switch the TV channel to YTV when Henry gets tired of the Disney Channel. I make him a peanut butter sandwich and one for myself as an afterthought. I have no money to buy dinner out and probably no chance of getting paid today. I perch on the edge of the couch, eating and tapping my foot impatiently, wishing Henry's mother would just get here already.

After a while Simon comes in from 318, where he's finally gotten all the crap off the walls. He's covered in spackle from patching holes. He stops by the door to kick off his work boots, which he keeps unlaced most of the time, then gives me a funny look.

"You have to pee or something?"

"No, why?"

"You're bouncing around like you've got spiders in your pants. You got someplace to be?"

I stop bouncing and stand up. My palms are actually sweating, and I wipe them on my jeans. "Yeah, I've got…" To go confront the man who ruined my family? No. Definitely not the approach to take. "…a party to go to. Marie-Claire invited me." What the hell: if it works for her, maybe it will work for me.

"Marie-Claire." Simon thinks that over for a second. "The scary goth chick who likes college boys? Gee, I can't see anything wrong with you going to a party with her."

"No, no." Damn it, I hadn't thought of it that way. Of course he's going to get all parental on me if he thinks there are going to be boys involved. True, I've been hanging around with Griffin my entire life, at least until this week, but Griffin hardly counts as a boy. "It's not one of *those* parties. It's, like…" Think! Think of something harmless! "…her little sister's first confession or something."

"First communion?"

"Maybe, I don't know. Some religious thing."

Simon lifts an eyebrow at me, suspicious. I try to think of the last time I tried to put one over on him and can't think of an occasion. There's a weird little knot in my stomach that I suppose might be guilt. I don't like lying to my brother. It's not just that I'm horrible at it, but he really doesn't deserve it. If it weren't for him, I'd be…well, in foster care, I suppose.

"How old is Marie-Claire's sister?" Simon asks.

I shrug. "Um, grade six? Maybe seven?"

"Then it's probably her confirmation. First communion is, like, grade two."

"Ah." The knot loosens a little. Maybe he wasn't suspicious after all. Maybe he just thinks I'm an idiot because I don't know anything about religion. Simon and Emily went to Catholic school when they were little, but Simon says Momma got a little ticked off at God or the Pope or something after Dad died and put me in public school out of spite.

"What time's the party?"

I glance down the hall at the clock in the kitchen. It's quarter after four.

"Five o'clock." Most businesses close at five o'clock, don't they? I'm hoping I&B Heating and Cooling isn't the sort of place where they knock off work early on a Friday afternoon. I don't think I can wait another two days to do this.

Simon sighs. "Well, let me get a shower and then I'll hang out with Henry so you can go to your party."

He holds up his index finger. "One time, you understand? This is not going to become a habit. I have enough work of my own to do around here."

"Deal." I almost jump up to give him a hug, but he's covered in dust and white goop. Besides, we're not really huggy people. If I act too excited to be getting out of baby-sitting to go to a twelve-year-old's church party, Simon really is going to get suspicious.

* * *

I have to run to catch the bus, my heart racing from nervous excitement and, let's face it, from the exertion as well. Too many years with Katie as my gym partner means I probably haven't spent nearly as much time running around as I ought to.

I&B Heating and Cooling is tucked away at the end of a dodgy-looking strip mall, next door to a boarded-up employment agency and two doors down from a nail salon. I get off the bus in front of the mall and pace up and down the sidewalk a couple of times. *Casing the joint.* I heard that in a movie once. I guess that's what I'm doing. There's a sign over the door with the company logo: a penguin wearing a parka, which looks like it might have been drawn by an eight-year-old. It's the same logo that's on the business card in my pocket, but somehow when it's all blown up big like this, it looks way cheesier. The shop has a glass door at the front that leads to a little reception area, where a heavyset blond girl with about half a dozen rings on her fingers and a dozen more piercing various parts of her face and ears is sitting. It looks like she's packing up for the day, stacking papers and tidying her desk. I pull out my cell phone to check the time: four fifty. If they close up at five, I don't have much time to find Travis. The parking lot wraps around the side of the building, where it joins up with the parking lot to another strip mall, this one with a women's gym and a pizza place. I see a van with the same cheesy cartoon penguin on the side parked around the back with its rear doors open.

"Jackpot," I hear myself say aloud. I recognize the older guy unloading toolboxes and bringing them into the building through a back door; he was at the hairdresser's with Travis.

"Hey, kid," he yells into the building. "You want to grab that extension cord for me?"

I freeze, a million thoughts running through my head. Who is this kid? Could he be talking about Travis? No way—Travis is in his thirties, way too old to be called a kid. Then again, when you're as old as this guy, maybe everyone under forty seems young. Or maybe Travis doesn't even work here anymore. Maybe he got fired, or violated his parole and got sent back to prison, or—and then, there he is. Dutifully fetching the extension cord from the truck, dressed in a grimy blue coverall and work boots, is the man himself, Travis Bingham.

I take a few steps toward him, pulling off my hat despite the cold wind. The first time I saw him, I was so bundled up he couldn't see much more than my nose, and the second, I was sitting in a hairdresser's chair at the back of the store while he stood in the reception area, not even looking in my direction. This time, I want him to really see me.

"I know who you are," I tell him.

Travis looks up, startled, squinting at me like I've woken him out of a deep sleep. We stand there for probably a full minute, just staring at each other. It suddenly occurs to me that I have no idea how dangerous he might be. How quick is his temper? Does he have it in for our entire family, not just my dad? If he suddenly attacks me and I scream, will anyone come running? But then a look of recognition washes over his face, and he even smiles a little.

"Emily?"

I scowl, shake my head. Not the reaction I was expecting. "No, I'm Jenna. Emily is my sister."

"Oh, wow. Right. Of course. You must be, what, sixteen?"

"I will be in October."

"Wow. Geez. How did you—?"

"Your picture was in the paper last week. I tracked you down from there."

He looks a little alarmed at that and lifts the huge extension cord up in front of him like a shield or something. "You tracked me down? Why would you do that?"

I suddenly think of being at the reptile show at the Festival of Friends with Simon when I was five or six. The toothless old guy running the booth had all kinds of snakes and turtles and iguanas you could pet, and a few spiders and other creatures that were just for looking at. One of those was a skittery little lizard who spent the whole time we were there scrambling around the back of its tank, trying to find a place to hide from all the kids tapping on the glass. I didn't want to go near it, but the toothless guy laughed at me and patted me on the head. "Don't worry, sweetie," he told me. "He's more scared of you than you are of him." That's what Travis reminds me of now, a rattled little gecko cowering in the back of a terrarium. More scared of me than I am of him.

"Don't worry, I'm not, um, out for revenge or anything. I just want to talk to you."

Travis looks at me for a long time, and I stare right back at him, thinking how much older he looks than Simon despite them being about the same age.

The East End is a tough enough neighborhood, but I guess Travis has spent the last fifteen years in an even tougher one. He looks…weary. Worn down. I feel like he's sizing me up, like the wheels are turning in his head as he tries to stare me down.

"Let me put this away and get changed," he says at last, tapping the extension cord with two fingers. "It's cold out here; we can go to the Tim's down on the corner and get a coffee."

"I don't drink coffee."

"Well, I'm sure they have some sort of alternative beverage on their menu." He smiles a little, nervous, awkward, and I can see what my mother meant about him having been a handsome boy.

I wait for him outside the shop, the cold stinging like a million little pinpricks running through my skin as the wind picks up again, whirling snowdrifts around the parking lot. Not for the first time, I wonder what on earth I've gotten myself into.

* * *

"So what do you want to know?"

Um, everything? How do I answer that question? I cup the hot chocolate that Travis bought for me despite my telling him three times that I was fine, I wasn't that thirsty, I didn't need anything to drink. He sips his coffee, staring at me over the rim of the cup as he lifts it to his lips.

"Why did you kill my dad?" I say finally.

Travis coughs a little, puts his hand to his nose like he's just snorted some coffee up it. "You want to say that a little quieter?" He looks around, jumpy, like he wants to make sure nobody's staring at us. They aren't—we're sitting in the corner by the bathrooms, where nobody else is sitting—but I can't say I'm too concerned whether he's comfortable or not.

"Well, why did you? I know you were pissed at him for throwing you out of our house, but murder seems a little...I don't know...extreme."

Travis presses his lips together so hard they turn white. "Jenna, I think maybe...I mean, you've got it wrong."

"What part do I have wrong?"

"I didn't"—he drops his voice down low, almost to a whisper—"I didn't kill him on purpose. I never meant for anybody to get hurt. He wasn't even supposed to be working that night."

I scowl. "Who was supposed to be working, then?"

Travis scowls, looks down at his coffee like it holds some great secret.

"This isn't entirely my story to tell, Jenna."

"Well, nobody else is going to tell it to me. I've been asking my brother for years, and he doesn't want to talk about it."

"What about your mom? Didn't she ever tell you what happened?"

I roll my eyes. "Are you kidding? My mom doesn't even know who I am ninety percent of the time."

"What do you mean?"

So I tell him the story of coming home and finding my mother in the bathroom, her brain scrambled beyond repair. Travis lets out a low whistle.

"That's…wow. I can't believe it. She was such a great person."

I shrug. "If you say so."

There's a long, awkward silence. Travis sips his coffee and studies his hands.

"Look, Jenna…maybe you should try asking Simon again. This is really…this is something he should be telling you."

"Why? Was he…" A terrible thought occurs to me suddenly. "Was he involved somehow?"

Travis hasn't seemed to be much on making eye contact to begin with, but now he doesn't even make any pretense of looking at me. "You…you really need to ask Simon."

"So that's a yes then. How?"

"Jenna, I—"

I take a look around the restaurant. There are maybe half a dozen customers besides the two of us, not to mention four or five people working behind the counter.

"Tell me. Or I'll scream. I swear."

That makes him look at me, really look at me, now. "Jesus, kid. You can't just let sleeping dogs lie? This whole thing…it was a lifetime ago."

I've heard variations of that line from Simon so many times, I just let it roll over me without comment. Instead I put on my best glare and fix it squarely on Travis.

"So what did my brother have to do with it?"

Travis looks as if it's taking every ounce of his strength to keep looking at me. His right eyelid twitches a little as he speaks.

"Simon was my best friend. He worked at the shop every Monday, Wednesday and Friday night. We had it all planned out. Your dad did all his banking on Tuesday mornings, like clockwork. So on Monday night I was going to burst in there with a mask and a gun, all *Point Break*, and Simon was going to empty out the safe. Except he wasn't there that night."

I sit there for a second, trying to process all of this. I run my thumb up and down the seam of the paper cup, hearing every sound in the coffee shop like someone has turned the volume up way too loud. I can hear the old guy at the counter ordering a large double-double; a couple of guys in security-guard uniforms two tables over complaining about their dispatcher; the girl behind the counter snapping her gum.

I want to ask him something smart, something that will make everything he just said make sense. Why did he want to rob my brother? What did he mean by *we*? And what the hell is *Point Break*? But the only thing I can force out of my mouth is "Why?"

"I don't know where he was that night. I thought it was going to be Simon when I burst through that door. I got the gun off this guy at school, um, Mike...what the hell was his name, Patterson, Parkinson, something like that. He was a real badass. Guns, knives, drugs...he could get you any of that. Twenty bucks. He said it was a piece of crap; said it wouldn't even fire. What do I know about guns, right?" He shrugs, makes this weird little sound that might be a laugh. "So here am I, wearing this Bill Clinton mask, bursting into Cooper's Smoke and Gift waving this gun around like I know what I'm doing with it, expecting Simon behind the counter, when all of a sudden your dad turns around. I was so surprised to see him, I probably jumped about a foot in the air. I didn't even hear the gun go off, but I must've squeezed the trigger because I sure felt it. I thought it had taken my arm clean off. It didn't even occur to me what was going on until I saw your dad hit the floor."

I suddenly wish I hadn't eaten that peanut butter sandwich. I can feel it sitting uneasily in my stomach as tears sting my eyes. "What did you do next?"

"I pulled off the mask, started freaking out—*Oh my god, Mr. Cooper, I'm so sorry, it was an accident…* I mean, ridiculous, right?" Travis laughs again, but there's no humor in it, none at all. "I tried to stop the bleeding, just leaned on him with my whole weight. I got him right here." He points to a spot right about the middle of his chest. "They said at the trial he never had a chance. The bullet nicked his aorta. There was so much blood." He bites his lip and stops talking, as if he was about to say something more. I'm not usually much of a crier, but as I listen to Travis talk I can feel tears running down my cheeks, and I use the heel of my hand to wipe them away.

"Was he dead? I mean, right away, when he hit the floor?"

Travis shakes his head. "No. He saw me when I took the mask off. He was staring right at me while I was trying to save him. I'll never forget the look in his eyes. That was pure hatred."

"Did he say anything?"

"He sure did." And he closes his mouth, lips pressed tight together in an odd grimace.

"Well? What did he say?"

"He said, 'You little bastard. I always knew you were no good.'" Travis's voice breaks a little, but he holds it together.

"You can see his point, though, can't you?" My own voice is steadier than I would have expected. "I mean, he takes you in after your own dad throws you out, and you repay him by robbing his store and shooting him."

I expect him to get defensive at that, raise his voice, get snippy at the very least, but instead he looks at me quizzically, a terrier with its head tilted to one side.

"Who told you that?"

"My momma." He's still staring at me like I've suddenly switched to speaking Portuguese or something, and I feel a strange urge to backpedal. "I mean…she's gone a little crazy since you saw her last, so sometimes she gets things kind of mixed up. But she told me your dad was this horrible guy who was always getting drunk and beating the crap out of you. In so many words. Is that… I mean, what part of it did she have wrong?"

Travis's voice, already quiet, gets even softer. "The part where it was *my* dad," he says. "My dad died in a car accident when I was twelve. And my mom never laid a hand on me either. I went to live with your family while my mom was in the hospital with breast cancer. Your mother was terrific. Said it was Christian charity, and I'd always been such a good friend to Simon. She wouldn't hear of me going anywhere else."

If my stomach was in knots before, it's now doing backflips and dancing the Macarena. I know the answer to my next question before I even ask it.

"So then, the raging, temperamental, abusive alcoholic Momma was talking about…"

"Was your dad, not mine," Travis finishes for me. There's a long silence while I try to process this new information. The happy sitcom family, the alternative reality I've always imagined for myself if only Travis Bingham hadn't ruined it for me, shatters as surely as if someone has thrown a rock through a TV screen. For an instant I consider the possibility that Travis is lying to me, but why would he? He doesn't even have to be here talking to me right now. What would he possibly have to gain by telling me that my dear, long-departed father was a drunken son of a bitch?

"But…" I struggle for words, trying to find my next question amid the wreckage of everything I've ever known about my past. "I still don't understand why you were… I mean, you were eighteen by the time my dad kicked you out, right? Why didn't you just…go away someplace? Was your mom still in the hospital?"

"No, she died." He says it like he's telling me the weather, but his eyes squint up a little, like it hurts to make the words come out of his mouth. "We wanted to get out of town. This guy Ben Astonberg—he used to work at this comic-book store up on Main near Queenston—he had an old K-car for sale. You probably don't even know what that is, do you? Talk about a piece of crap. He wanted six hundred bucks for it. We were gonna take it out west someplace, get jobs in Alberta or something, get as far away from David Cooper and Hamilton, Ontario, as that old piece of junk would carry us."

"We?" I echo, still feeling like I'm missing something.

Travis gives me that confused-terrier look again, like he's not sure how I could possibly be this dense.

"Me and Simon," he says. "The whole robbery thing was his idea."

"I…he…what?" I shake my head emphatically. "No. That's impossible."

"He thought it would be the perfect crime. Your dad had video cameras all over his store, I think as much to make sure Simon wasn't stealing anything from him as to prevent shoplifting. Not that Simon was the type to steal. Or do anything out of line, really. He just didn't have it in him, you know? A real straight arrow. Honor roll, debate club. And smart. Man, that guy was smart.

We all figured he'd wind up a lawyer or a doctor or something. Rich, famous, the works. He was a year younger than me, but he was taking all OAC classes—that's like a level above grade twelve. I don't even think they have those anymore, do they?"

I shake my head. "No. Not in a long time. It just goes up to grade twelve now."

Travis barely takes notice of my answer though. He's on a roll, like he needs to get the rest of the story out now that he's started telling it. "Simon was going to be the guy where you'd say 'Hey, I knew him back when.' But he came over one night, probably like a week before you were born, and he'd had enough. He'd caught the raw end of your dad's temper one too many times, and he had a black eye coming up. I was staying at a place just off Parkdale, renting a room off this old couple and cleaning ashtrays in a pool hall nights while I finished up high school. Simon came up with this plan, and it sounded like the perfect crime. I'd go in wearing a mask, get an old coat from the Goodwill or something so your dad wouldn't recognize me on the videotape. We'd pick a night when Simon was working and there was lots of cash in the safe. He'd act scared, hand over all the money…and who'd be able to blame him? Clearly there was a crazy guy with a gun: what else would he do? We were gonna stash the money, wait until semester break in January and off we'd go. Only it didn't work out that way, obviously."

"Why would you wait, if you had the money to leave?"

Travis actually smiles at that. "Your brother was such a nerd. At the end of the semester he'd have had enough credits to graduate, so he could take college courses out west. He figured he could stick it out a couple more months if we at least had a nest egg and a plan to escape."

"So what happened, then? Why wasn't Simon there that night?"

Travis shrugs. "Your guess is as good as mine. I never got a chance to ask him. Haven't seen him since."

I'm reeling, feeling faint. I put my head down on the table to stop it from spinning, staring down at the scratched-up laminate because it feels like I'm going to pass out if I get one more piece of information right now. *It serves you right,* I can hear Simon's voice saying in my head. *You're the one who wanted answers. Now you've got them: what are you going to do next?*

"Jenna?" Travis puts his hand on my shoulder, gently, tentatively, like he's not real used to touching other people. "Jenna, are you okay?"

I lift my head to glare back at him, my eyes stinging with tears. "Yeah. Yeah, I'm just great. How else would I be?" I take a swig of my hot chocolate, which has finally dropped below the temperature of molten lava, and push it away from me. "Listen, Travis, thanks for the talk, but I really have to get going."

I try to push my chair back, then realize it's the kind of chair that's bolted to the floor, so instead of the suave exit I was going for, I wind up looking like I'm having some kind of spasm. I've been fighting back the tears the whole time Travis has been talking, chewing my lower lip until I taste blood. Now, though, I utterly lose it, and I start to sob uncontrollably. I can't remember the last time I cried, and it feels…painful. Awkward. I can feel everyone in the restaurant turning to stare at me.

"Jenna, look, I'm really sorry…"

But I don't let him finish. I don't care if he's sorry. No, that's not true. I'm glad he's sorry. He's as sorry as a person can be, I guess. You don't get much sorrier than Travis Bingham. But somehow that seems irrelevant to me now.

I slide out of my chair, a little more gracefully this time, and stumble out of the Tim Hortons. The girl behind the counter gets a look at me, mouths "Are you okay?" as I pass by. I nod, snotty-nosed and bleary-eyed, and step out into the dark, freezing cold of the parking lot.

I stand in the bus shelter, which at least slows down the wind, and pull my cell phone out of my pocket. I angle it back and forth in the light from the streetlamp across the street, trying frantically to find Ashley's number in my directory. I can't go home right now, now that I know Simon is the one responsible for everything I'd always blamed on Travis Bingham. Even if my dad was as bad as Travis said, or worse, what the hell am I going to say to Simon now? I need a friendly place to fall, and since I seem to be running low on those lately, Ashley is my only option at the moment.

It occurs to me that, although she's been to my apartment, I don't have the faintest clue where she lives. Even if I wanted to just show up on her doorstep out of the blue, I wouldn't be able to. I scroll through the few numbers on my list: Griffin's cell, Griffin's home, Katie's cell, Katie's home, Marie-Claire's home—she's the only person I know who doesn't have a cell. I've gone through the list three times before I realize Ashley's number isn't there. Damn it! I think hard: when did we exchange numbers, anyway? It was after gym class a couple of days ago, mine scrawled hastily and hers etched neatly in big, round, girly writing on one of those pamphlets they have sitting in a little plastic display attached to the wall outside the girls' change room— *Sexually Transmitted Infections and You* or *What You Need To Know About Illegal Drugs and Alcohol* or *Pregnant? Need To Talk?* or something equally distressing. I tucked the half of the pamphlet with Ashley's number into the outside pocket of my backpack and…left it there. And my backpack is at home, sitting in the front hall of my apartment, exactly where I don't want to—where I *can't* be right now.

I catch the next bus that comes by, not even caring where it's going. It's one of the long, bendy buses that looks like it's got a big accordion in the middle. I flash the driver my bus pass and find a seat about three-quarters of the way back. I sit sideways on the seat, tilting my head back so the top of my skull is pressed up against the window as hard as it can be. It feels like my head is going to explode, and the pressure from the window seems to help, at least for a minute or two.

I've never been on this bus route before, and once we get off the main drag, I don't recognize anything. This part of town looks like a whole different world from the one I live in. There are vast expanses of parkland, and half-built houses that look like mansions compared to our old family home on Province Street. I think about all the perfect little families that will move into them, living their perfect little lives. I feel like a spy in a foreign country, but now I'm a spy without a mission. I've tracked down my target; I've completed my task, and all I feel is…empty. Now what do I do?

The bus stops here and there, letting one or two people off or on at a stop. I'm used to seeing the hordes of lost souls that wait in the shelters along the B-Line to cram aboard, so it's weird to see so few people taking the bus. I guess all those double garages are full of suvs and minivans, so nobody needs public transportation up here.

I ride the entire way around the route, finally coming back to the bus shelter by the Tim Hortons where I first got on. The bus stops, lets off a woman in a brown visor who looks like she's starting her shift at Timmy's. I think about getting off, but I can't think where else to go. I stay on the bus for a long time, and finally the driver pulls over at a stop and comes back to talk to me.

"You okay, sweetheart? You know where you're going?"

I blink, startled. "Uh, yeah. No. I…um…" Can't think of a good lie. "I thought this bus went back downtown."

He's an old guy—grandfatherly, I guess. Not that I would know. My dad left all his family back in Ireland when he came to Canada, and my mom's parents were both dead before I was born. "Not this one, honey. Come sit up at the front; I'll tell you where to get off to transfer."

"Okay." My voice sounds very small. "Thanks."

He directs me off the #44 and onto the #11, down Parkdale and back into familiar territory. The intersection where I get off is shared by an adult video store and an elementary school. I stand with my arms crossed for a minute, hands tucked under my arms to warm them up, before I head across the street to catch the #3.

I have to wait for a few minutes, wondering if I'm really heading in the right direction. But with no money and no place else to go, I don't really have much choice. My heart is racing as the bus pulls up and I step aboard.

"Cold night," says the driver, a heavyset woman with thick glasses. I pull out my bus pass again, fingers stiff from the cold.

"It sure is."

I catch a glimpse of myself in the driver's mirror as I take a seat near the front of the bus. I look like a wreck: hair tangled from the wind, my eyes red and bleary. I'm the only one on the bus except for an emo-looking kid sitting right at the back, with an army-green toque pushing out bangs so long you can't see his eyes. He's got his iPod turned up so loud I can hear the bass line from the front of the bus. He's bopping his head along with the beat, not a care in the world.

I tug the cord and the *Next Stop* light at the front of the bus turns on. I step out into the cold and look around, checking for crazies. There's a homeless guy down the block, shuffling up and down the sidewalk in front of a discount muffler place, mumbling to himself, but he looks mostly harmless. I'm not going that far anyway. I cross the street and climb the steps to the crooked old white house that has been my second home since I was about five years old. It looks more foreboding than it ever has before, and I've never been so nervous about knocking on the door. But it's this or freeze to death out here, and both options seem more viable than going home right now. I have to knock a couple of times before I hear footsteps on the stairs, and I wonder if anyone is even going to open the door. It's not like they're expecting me, after all.

"Who's there?" asks a voice through the door.

"Ms. Quinn? Is Katie here?"

"Oh, Jenna." She sounds relieved. I wonder if the guy down by the muffler place has been wandering around for long enough to have freaked her out. "Katie's at work, but of course you're welcome to come in and wait."

"Thanks." I step inside, take off my shoes and coat.

"I'm making supper for Katie, but there's lots. Would you like some?"

Now that I think of it, that peanut butter sandwich was a long time ago. Plus, it's not wise to turn down a free meal when you don't know where your next one is coming from. I can't even imagine going home again right now. I'm thinking about worst-case scenarios, wondering if I'm going to be homeless, if they'll let me into a shelter or put me in a group home or something. I wonder about the crazy guy down the street, whether he was crazy before he was homeless or if being homeless was what put him over the edge.

"I'd love some supper," I say, forcing a polite smile.

Whether she notices I've been crying or not, Ms. Quinn doesn't say anything. I guess she figures that whatever's going on, there's no problem a plate of pork chops and mashed potatoes can't solve. On an ordinary day, I'd almost be inclined to agree with her. She's a heck of a good cook. Katie's still not home by the time I finish my dinner, and I ask if I can wait for Katie in her room.

"I can't imagine that would be a problem," says Katie's mom, and away I go.

I flop down into Katie's beanbag chair and pick up a magazine. Not a normal magazine, like *People* or *Seventeen*, but *Time*. I flip through articles about why kids these days are so fat, how bad the economy is, all sorts of depressing crap. I guess things are rough all over. I suppose I should buck up and stop feeling sorry for myself, but I'm finding it hard to see past the fact that my brother is, for all intents and purposes, a murderer.

* * *

It's another half hour or so before Katie gets home, and I hear her talking to her mother downstairs—not the actual words, just muffled voices through the floor. I can hear a whining note in Katie's voice, then a plaintive "You let her in my *room*?" that rises above the ambient noise of the furnace chugging away.

I feel a twinge of—what? Guilt? Self-righteous indignation? I have so much running through my head right now that I can't even tell what I'm feeling. I hear Katie on the stairs, the floor shuddering as she storms up them. She flings open the door, scowling deeply as she looks around the room, her gaze coming to rest on me in the beanbag.

"What the hell—" She breaks off when she sees my face.

"You were right," I tell her, my voice cracking. "I should have just left things alone."

Katie looks alarmed. She sits on the bed. "What happened?"

"It was Simon." And in one breath, I pour out the whole story. Katie sits in silence through it all, her mouth open, eyes like Frisbees. I tell her everything, from meeting Travis on Saturday to getting off the bus by her house tonight. When I'm finished, she lets out a whistle.

"Wow. I'm really sorry."

"Yeah." I trail the heel of my hands across my eyes. "Me too."

"I mean, here we were telling you to leave well enough alone, but you knew there was something more to it the whole time, didn't you?"

I shrug. "Yeah, I guess."

"Wow, we had it all wrong. I'm so sorry. I mean, no wonder you were so obsessed."

I suppose I should feel some sort of…what? Vindication? But I don't, really. I don't think I've been poking around all these years because I had some sort of sixth sense, I just…I don't know. Needed to feel some sort of connection to the father I never had. Momma always talked about him like he was some kind of saint, but I guess she figured telling me the truth about him would be adding insult to injury. I mean, he went and got himself murdered; did she really need to point out that he was a complete jerk as well? And the newspaper articles that talked about his murder said he was this great guy too, but what else were they going to say? That he was a terrible person and deserved what he got? Of course not.

I lean back against the wall, look up at the light fixture on Katie's ceiling. It looks like a glass dish with two light-bulbs in it. It hangs down a couple of inches from the ceiling, and in the summer it's always got a couple of dead flies sitting in it.

"Do you think…" I stare harder at the light fixture, not wanting to look right at Katie. I don't really want to look at anybody right now. "Do you think your mom would let me stay here for a few days?" My voice breaks a little bit. "I just don't think I can go home."

"Are you sure you want to stay with me? I mean, I thought Ashley Walsh was your new best friend." She doesn't sound spiteful, just…matter-of-fact.

I shrug. "Ashley's fine. But…" I figure it would be prudent to leave out the fact that I couldn't find her phone number and don't know where she lives. "I just haven't known her that long. I thought maybe you'd understand what a big deal this is."

I don't have any particular gift for saying the right thing at the right time, but I think in this case I may have succeeded. It probably wouldn't serve my interests at this point to remind her that *she* was the one who dropped *me* like a hot rock.

"I'll check with my mom," Katie says. "I don't think she'll have a problem with it." She turns on the TV. "You want to watch *Cosby* or something?"

Happy families, working it all out. "No thanks. I don't believe in that stuff anymore."

Katie gives me a funny look but flips through the channels accommodatingly. We skip past *Law & Order*—

I'm not in the mood for a murder mystery now that I've solved one of my own—and finally settle on one of those home-decorating shows where people spend more money on a couch than most of the people in my apartment building make in a month. It's a nice distraction from talking about the real world, though, and we sit there in silence until Katie's mother brings up her supper and a plate of home-baked muffins for us.

"Mom, can Jenna sleep over?"

Ms. Quinn gives me a big smile. "Of course. It's always nice to have company."

And it's that easy.

Katie's mom hauls out an inflatable bed from the basement and finds me some sheets. Katie and I actually have a few laughs as we blow up the air mattress, which feels pretty good considering the evening I've had. Ms. Quinn makes up the bed for me like she's spreading out fine linens for the Queen or something.

"Do you girls want some chips or a drink? I think there's still a bottle of Coke in the fridge."

"No thanks," I tell her. Good grief, I'm going to weigh five hundred pounds by Sunday if I don't start saying no.

After an hour or two of lying around watching tv, Katie on her bed and me on the air mattress, we decide to turn off the light and go to sleep. I've slept over at Katie's countless times—never her at my place, always me at hers—and it's never like the sleepovers you see in movies, with pillow fighting and talking about boys. It's always just sitting around watching TV until we get tired and then going to sleep. But tonight, once the light is off, I suddenly feel more like talking.

"The thing that gets me," I say into the darkness, "is that I've asked Simon about my dad, like, once a week since I realized I didn't have one."

"Uh-huh."

I can't tell from that uh-huh whether Katie wants me to shut up or keep talking, so I choose the latter. "If he'd even just once said, 'Our dad was a complete dick,' maybe I would have given up on this whole thing."

"Maybe he just didn't want to speak ill of the dead. Or he feels guilty."

"Well, he ought to feel guilty! He killed his father! Well, as good as, anyway."

There's a long silence, and then Katie asks, "So what was he like?"

"Who, my dad?"

"No, Travis. Was he scary? Did he freak out when he saw you?"

"No. He wasn't scary at all. He was just…" I think it over for a second. "He was just a guy, you know? He actually thought I was Emily at first."

"Well, you do look a lot like her. I mean, what she must have looked like when she was fifteen. She looks even older than Simon now. But think about it. Travis was gone for fifteen years. He probably remembers Emily when she was, what, nine years old?"

"Eight."

"Right. I bet you would lose track of time, being in prison for so long."

I wonder about that for a minute. "I don't think I would. Especially if I were Travis. I think I would spend every day counting off the minutes until I got out. I mean, he shouldn't have been the one in there, really. Or at least he shouldn't have been in there alone. Simon should have been with him."

There's a long silence, and I wonder if maybe Katie has fallen asleep, but finally she responds. "If Simon was in prison, where would that have left you? And Wex? And Emily? I mean, it's not like Simon has spent the whole fifteen years out partying or something."

I chew on that for a while. It's true: Simon doesn't really have a great life. When was the last time he even *went* to a party? Or had a date? Or worked at a job that didn't completely suck? Even before we lived with him, he was still over at our house almost every day, checking up on Momma, making sure she'd remembered to feed us, buying diapers for Wex when Emily forgot, helping me with my homework. I think about what Travis said, about Simon having always been the smart one, the responsible one. He should have been a doctor or a lawyer or something, not someone who cleans up other people's crap for a living. Has he spent his entire life trying to make up for that one—huge, granted, yes, but only one—mistake?

I lie there in the dark for a long time, thinking about how many little things had to go wrong for that one horrible thing to happen. I wonder how often Simon thinks about it, about what else he could have been. Another year and he could have been gone. But then... where would I be? Stuck in a house with a psycho who drinks and beats up his kids, I suppose. I wonder if Momma would have gone nuts anyway, even if Dad hadn't died. Would Emily still have had Wex? Somehow I doubt she'd have been better adjusted than she is with a father like that. I just lie there and listen to the cars go by outside, wondering and wondering, hearing Katie start to snore. Finally, after an eternity, I drift away into the darkness myself and let sleep catch up with me.

* * *

It barely feels like I've been asleep when Katie's mother knocks on her door.

"Jenna, honey?"

"Mmf?" I sit up, groggy, pushing my hair out of my face.

"Jenna, did you forget to ask your brother if you could sleep over?"

"Sorry, what?" It takes me a minute to remember where I am and why. At least I don't need to act like I don't know what she's talking about.

"Your brother, sweetie. He's on the phone. He wanted to know if you were here. The poor boy—he's worried sick."

I'm on the verge of telling her that "the poor boy" is only about five years younger than she is but figure that might sound rude. "I could have sworn I left him a note," I mumble instead.

"He must not have seen it. I told him you're fine, but he wants to talk to you."

She hands me the cordless phone and I put it up to my ear. "Hello?"

I've never heard such an explosion out of Simon as the one that comes out of the phone. "What the hell has gotten into you lately?" I sense the question is rhetorical so I just shrug, not quite awake enough to realize he can't see me through the phone. I hold the phone a little farther away from my ear—he's really screaming at me. I'm just hearing highlights of his monologue. "Called Marie-Claire…didn't know what I was talking about…lying…felt like an idiot…"

"Look, it's, um—" I look from Katie, still snoring away, to her mother, concerned and, well, motherly, standing in the doorway. "It's really late. Can we talk about whatever I did or didn't do in the morning?"

There's a long silence. I don't know what kind of reaction Simon was looking for, but whatever it was, it's not what I just gave him. I picture him deflating into a shriveled mess on the floor, like a big Mylar balloon that's been punctured, and it feels oddly satisfying.

"Fine," he says finally and hangs up. If we had one of those old-fashioned phones at home, with the handset and cord, I'm sure he would be slamming the receiver down in a huff. As it is, though, all he'll be able to do is press the Off button with what will be an unsatisfying little *bleep*.

I do the same on my end and hand the phone back to Ms. Quinn. "I'm sorry about all that."

"It's okay, sweetie. Sometimes big brothers are a pain, aren't they?" She gives me a little smile, but with the hallway light shining behind her, it's hard to see if she's being sympathetic or patronizing.

"Yeah, they can be."

"Do you want to go back to sleep? Or would you like some hot chocolate or something?"

"No, thank you. I'm not thirsty."

It's not hard to see how Katie got to be as big as she is. Every time something comes up that might be hard to talk about, her mother offers her food. It figures that Katie deals with every little problem she has by eating.

"All right then," Ms. Quinn tells me. "Have a great sleep."

I don't, after that. I'm not sure what time it was when Simon called, but the rest of the night drags on endlessly. I toss and turn on the air mattress, my body exhausted but my brain going a mile a minute.

I suppose I must have fallen asleep at some point, because I startle awake to find the sun streaming through the window and Katie shuffling around her room, getting dressed.

"Oh hey, sorry, I thought you were asleep." Katie pulls the blanket off her bed and uses it to cover up. I roll over and close my eyes, pretending to go back to sleep even though she's probably not fooled. Katie's not big on public nudity, so I'll accommodate her by pretending I saw nothing.

Once she's dressed, Katie flops down on the bed and I make a big production of pretending to wake up. I stretch and sit up.

"How long have you been up? What time is it?"

"I don't know. Long enough to have a shower, I guess." Katie finds her cell phone on her bedside table and checks the time. "It's eight fifty-one. Why, do you have someplace to be?"

"Nowhere at all. Hey, can I grab a shower?"

"Yeah. You can borrow some of my mom's clothes, if you want. They'd probably fit you better than mine."

Katie tiptoes into her mother's room—her mom is still sleeping—and comes back with a T-shirt and sweatpants and a pair of wool socks. I'm glad that's all she's brought. It's odd enough to be borrowing a friend's mother's clothes, never mind underwear. I just wear my own from yesterday for the time being. Maybe I can sneak into the apartment later and pack some clothes.

When I'm clean and dressed, Katie and I head downstairs to forage for food. She opens a cupboard to reveal a shelf of cereal boxes. I've never seen anything like it. We've never had more than one box of cereal in our house at a time. There are neon colors and all manner of flavors and smiling cartoon characters on the boxes, the contents guaranteed to have no nutritional value whatsoever.

"This is awesome." I've never had anything more exotic than no-name frosted flakes, and I'm having a hard time deciding between the box with the grinning bear or the one with the goofy leprechaun. Both seem to involve some sort of colored marshmallows. In the end, I decide to have a small bowl of the fruity bear cereal, then follow it up with a bowl of the leprechaun cereal.

I haven't even had a chance to get a bowl out of the cupboard when there's a knock on the door.

"That's weird." Katie goes to answer it. "It's probably the Jehovah's Witnesses or something."

I follow her, Ms. Quinn's wool socks skidding a little on the freshly polished wood floors. "Or the what-do-you-call-them, the ones with the suits and name tags. Morons."

Katie finds that hilarious. "Mor*mon*s, you idiot."

"Whatever. I don't know one guy with religious pamphlets from another."

I poke my head around the corner so I can see the front hall, just in case it's the freaky homeless guy who was wandering up and down the street last night. It's not though. There, standing at Katie's door, his arms crossed over his chest and his gloveless hands tucked into his armpits for warmth, is Simon.

"You." He looks past Katie to where I'm standing. There are bags under his eyes and a frown line like an exclamation point over each eyebrow. "Go and get in the truck. Now."

Katie turns and looks back at me, her eyes wide. I must confess I'm a little alarmed myself. I've seen Simon annoyed before, but never really mad. The look on his face now tells me he's miles from fooling around.

"What are you going to do?" Katie hisses at me, her back to Simon. I shrug. He doesn't know I know anything—at this point, he's just mad that I lied to him and stayed out overnight without telling him. But that's nothing compared with how angry I am at him for lying to me for fifteen years. If he wants to yell at me, that's fine; I've got some yelling of my own to do. And it's not like he's *dangerous*, despite being sort of a killer. I mean, it's *Simon*. Then again…I look at his face, the twitching muscle along his jawline as he clenches his teeth and stares me down.

"*Now*, Jenna."

I chew on my lip a little. I don't see any way out of this house without going past Simon, and he's a lot bigger than I am.

"I need to get my clothes," I tell him. "They're upstairs."

"Hurry up."

I contemplate making a run for it, out the back door, but I suspect there's a sizable snowdrift up against it that would make it impossible to open. Instead I just head up to Katie's room, taking my sweet time, and grab the bundle of clothes I left rolled in a little ball on her

187

bedroom floor. I'm somehow hungry and nauseated at the same time as I trudge back downstairs.

Katie grabs my arm on my way out. "Call me later, okay?"

"Definitely."

It's warmer outside than I expect, and the wet feel of the air makes me wonder if it's going to snow again. I climb into the cab of Simon's pickup truck and fasten my seatbelt. My stomach rumbles, and I think about my missed opportunity for breakfast.

"What the hell is the matter with you lately?" Simon gets in, slams his door behind him. His face is purple, and I can see a vein bulging at his temple. "I called Marie-Claire when you didn't come home. There was no party. Why the hell would you just make something like that up? If you wanted to sleep over at Katie's, you could have slept over at Katie's—why would I say no?"

I shrug. "It was kind of spur-of-the-moment, I guess."

"What does that even mean? Damn it, Jenna, I would expect this kind of crap from Emily. What's the matter with you? You're skipping school, you're bailing on work, you're lying to me every chance you get. What the hell is going on?"

"I've been...um...busy."

Simon's eyebrows fly up his forehead. He lets out a weird little cough. "*Busy*? What's that supposed to mean? Is there a boy in the picture? Are you on drugs?"

"No. But I…had to go out with somebody last night."

"With who?"

I sit for a minute, staring out the window at Cannon Street. It's quiet on a Saturday morning, nobody to be seen. I wonder again what became of the mumbling homeless guy from last night. I don't know what to say to Simon. This isn't how I saw this confrontation happening. I wanted…what? The upper hand? Control of the conversation? That's it. And I don't have it.

After a long while of sitting with the truck in park and Simon trying to stare a hole through the back of my skull, I turn around to face him. "I'm hungry," I say, scowling back at him. "I never got a chance to eat breakfast."

Simon lets out a sigh. I'm winning again. "There's food at home. You can eat after you tell me what the hell's gotten into you."

"No." I suspect his rage level is nothing compared to mine right now, and I'm determined to get the upper hand back. "I want to go to Bedrock Bistro. And I'm *not* going home right now. If you try to make me, I'll…well, I just won't. That's all."

Simon's death glare is pretty impressive, but mine is better. After a minute or so of staring at him, he lets out a hiss.

"Fine," he says and starts the truck.

I've never been to Bedrock Bistro before, but I pass by it all the time. It's got pictures of Fred Flintstone and the gang out front and a leaderboard that says stuff like *Best Eggs Benedict In Hamilton*. I don't know what eggs benedict is, but this has been a week for trying new things. I've skipped school, gotten a makeover, eaten shawarma, been an accomplice to auto theft—or, at least, auto borrowing-without-permission—tracked down a murderer and made a new friend. Or maybe even two. Not like I'll be hanging out with Travis Bingham anytime soon, but he's not such a bad guy, all things considered. And who knows? Maybe shooting my dad was the best thing anyone could have done for me. Emily only lived with him for eight years, and look how screwed up she is.

Simon drives us to the restaurant. His face has gone from purple back to its regular pink, although his ears are still pretty red, so he's clearly still fuming. The little parking lot is crowded on a Saturday morning, but Simon manages to catch a car just backing out of a spot and pulls in as it's leaving.

We get a booth in the back. There are TVs everywhere playing episodes of *The Flintstones*. Simon orders coffee and I get a big glass of chocolate milk, and neither of us says anything to each other for a long time. I can tell Simon's waiting for me to talk, like there's nothing else for him to say. I wait until the waitress comes with our drinks, though, and order my eggs benedict.

Simon looks like he's ready to explode, but he's not the type to make a scene in public. Yet another reason why I'd rather have this conversation in a crowded restaurant. I suppose I should just spit it out, already.

"I couldn't tell you where I went last night because I was going to meet Travis Bingham."

There. I've got it out there. If Simon were a cartoon character, his eyes would have popped right out of his head with an *arooga* sound like they always do on TV. He sputters, and I can't help but feel like we're in one of the *Flintstones* episodes playing on the TVs all over this place. "But—where did you? How? Why would…"

"I saw in the paper that he was out of prison. It wasn't that hard to find him, really. I'm pretty clever when I want to be. And he had quite a story to tell me."

Simon's face has changed color again. He's whiter than Marie-Claire when she's in her full vampire goth-girl getup. "I can imagine," he says, his voice suddenly very small.

"I'm actually surprised you didn't know he was back in town, seeing as you were such good friends. But the thing I don't get is, if you were as good a friend as he says you were, how come he hasn't seen you in fifteen years?

I'd think you might have written him a letter or something, seeing as how the whole thing was your idea."

Simon opens his mouth like he's going to say something, clamps it shut instead and then opens it again, his brow furrowing. Finally he takes a sip of his coffee, I presume to gather his composure, and then presses his lips together so tightly the color drains out of them. "I wasn't allowed to see Travis," he says finally. "It was a condition of my probation."

Now it's my turn to gape at him like a perplexed goldfish. "You got probation?"

"Yeah. Travis left that part out of the story he told you, huh? Well, fair enough. The judge figured I'd suffered enough and let me plead guilty to Mischief Endangering Life, and I got a year of probation. I was seventeen, so I don't even have a criminal record anymore. Travis was a year older, so he was tried as an adult. He's the one who really got shafted."

"Well, Dad didn't make out so well in that whole situation either."

Simon sighs. "Jenna, Dad wasn't exactly—"

"I know. Travis told me. He was a drunken asshole. But I'm pretty sure that's not a capital offense."

"It was more than that, Jenna. You don't know what it was like, having to walk on eggshells all the time. You never knew whether he was gonna come home with a big smile on his face and presents for everybody, or whether he was going to storm in and beat the crap out of anybody who stepped in his way."

"Did he beat up Emily and Mom too, or was it just you?"

I see a little muscle twitch under Simon's left eye. "Mom got the worst of it when I was little. If the house wasn't clean enough, if dinner wasn't what he felt like eating on a particular night, all hell broke loose. Emily managed to stay out of his way most of the time, but she was always right there, watching everything he did to her. And…me. By the time I was in high school, he'd pretty much given up on Mom to focus on me." He has a strange look in his eyes, like he's staring straight through me and back into another time.

"Travis told me you were supposed to be the one working that night, but you never showed up. Why—"

"Hang on." Simon gestures for me to stop talking as the waitress arrives with our breakfast. Simon, adventurous as always, has two eggs over hard and a side of bacon. He digs in like he hasn't seen food in a week. He's probably hoping I'll be too busy with my eggs benedict—which isn't as exotic as I thought it would be: just eggs and ham on an english muffin with some kind of goop all over it, although the goop is pretty delicious—to press him for more information.

"So where were you, then?" I ask again after a few bites of goopy egg.

Simon looks…I don't know. Embarrassed? "I was at home. I was supposed to be at work at five, and I was so jazzed about this stupid plan we had—we'd been talking about it for weeks, and here it was, finally happening. But my stomach was all in knots, I guess from nerves, so I went to the bathroom and threw up. I felt better right after, but doesn't Dad walk in and see me getting sick."

"Yeah, so?"

"So he figured I had the flu or something and told me to go to bed, he'd cover my shift for me." He lets out a snort. "First nice thing he ever did for me, and look how it turned out."

"And you couldn't call Travis and tell him not to come?"

"I tried, believe me. But this was fifteen years ago; it wasn't like everybody had cell phones. Travis had already left, and I couldn't sneak out and head him off at the pass because Mom was home. I was hoping he'd walk by first and notice Dad was there, but…" He shrugs, leaves the thought unfinished and takes another bite of egg.

I watch him chewing, letting everything he's told me sink in. But there's one thing still bothering me. "So if Dad was such a horrible person, why didn't anyone ever tell me?" I want to know.

Simon shrugs. His color has pretty much returned to normal—pasty and freckled. "Emily and I talked about that once, and Momma too, back before…you know, the *thing*."

The *thing*. That's a nice way of saying *the time she took a bunch of pills and tried to drown herself in the bathtub.* "And what did you decide when you talked about it?"

"We thought, you know, you had this little fantasy about this amazing daddy that you never got to have. And you know, it was kind of nice. Like, he got to be a better person after he died than he was when he was alive, even if it was only in your imagination. Why would we want to spoil that?"

"I can't decide if I'm flattered or insulted by that."

Simon shrugs. "When in doubt, be flattered, I guess. But you just wouldn't leave things alone. It was like you were determined to just keep picking and picking at it until you found out what was underneath."

"And now I have."

He lets out a sigh. "Now you have."

I finish my chocolate milk and take another bite of egg as I try to figure out what comes next. So Simon didn't get away scot-free after all. All these years, and I was the only one who didn't know.

"So Travis said you were really smart."

Simon gives me a funny look. "And, what, now I'm stupid?"

"No, not…especially. But you could probably do a lot better than you have been."

He pulls an odd face, like he's setting his jaw. I recognize that expression: I make it myself when I'm being stubborn. "I do okay," he says.

"No you don't. You clean up after crackheads and chase welfare bums around for rent. And to make matters worse, it's not like you get to drive home to a nice house on the Mountain at the end of the day. You have to *live* with them."

"Well, what else am I supposed to do? I barely finished high school—that's all I've got."

"So finish something else. You're thirty-two—it's not like you're sixty-five and ready to retire. Get a girlfriend. Get a hobby. Quit beating yourself up and go get a life."

Simon looks startled, then laughs. Actually, really laughs. "You should get a job as a motivational speaker. Just go up onstage and call everybody a loser and tell them to go get a life."

"I call it like I see it. You big wiener."

"You're a jerk, you know that?"

"Yeah, but I'm your jerk and you're stuck with me."

He shakes his head, a little half-smile crossing his lips. "Finish your eggs, you twerp."

* * *

It's noon when we get home, and Simon goes down to the basement to get his cleaning stuff. He's behind, which he reminds me jokingly is entirely my fault.

Wex is sprawled out on the couch playing Tekken. When I come in, he barely looks up from digitally beating the crap out of some anime guy in a loincloth.

"Where's your mom?" I ask him.

"Taking a nap. She has to work tonight."

I sit down beside him. "Did you eat breakfast?"

"Yeah, Mom made pancakes. Aw." He throws down his controller. "You just made me die again."

"Yeah, sorry about that. But seriously? Emily made… food?"

"Yeah. She works in a restaurant, you know." He sounds a little defensive.

"She washes dishes."

Wex shrugs. "So? She's learning to cook too."

Wow. Emily's sober, she's paying attention to her son, she's got a job. Will wonders never cease?

"So it sounds like she's doing okay, huh?" I say.

"Yeah, I guess so. And I like her boyfriend, too."

"Yeah? You think he's the real deal?"

"Yeah, they've been going out for a few weeks now. His name is Dave. He works with her."

"*Dave?* Dave the *waiter?*" I start to laugh.

"Yeah. So what?"

"She's dating Dave the waiter?" I'm hysterical by this point, laughing so hard there are tears in my eyes.

"Yeah. So what? What's funny?"

"Nothing. Nothing at all." I wipe my eyes with the heels of my hands. I don't even know why I find that so amusing. "I'm sure he's very nice."

"He is. He came to McDonald's with us yesterday. He says he's going to take me fishing in the spring."

"That's awesome. It really is." I throw an arm around Wex and give him a kiss on top of his head. "It's just…it's funny the way life works out sometimes, isn't it?"

"I guess." He ducks out from under my arm and picks up his game controller again. "I mean, whatever doesn't kill you makes you stronger, right?"

"What? Where did you hear that?"

He shrugs. "tv," he says.

"Of course you did."

I leave Wex to beat up the guy in his computer game and head off to my room. I flop down on the chair in the corner and dig out the sweater I've been knitting for Simon. As infuriating as he can be, he really is a decent guy, I guess.

TWO MONTHS LATER

I'm the last one to finish my lunch—leftover Chinese food Emily brought home from the restaurant—and I slide my Rubbermaid lunch container into my backpack and look up to find everyone staring at me.

"Oh, were you all waiting for me?"

"Yeah, little Miss Gourmet." Griffin had a peanut butter sandwich today, and the whole time I was eating, I could see him out of the corner of my eye, coveting my cold chicken wings and chow mein.

"All right, who was the asshole yesterday?"

"I think it was Griffin," says Katie.

"Griffin's always the asshole," chimes in Ashley.

"Very funny." Griffin pulls his deck of cards out of his backpack and shuffles. He makes a big production of it. "This is the faro shuffle. It looks simple, but it's very tricky." He drops about fifteen cards on the floor.

"How about I shuffle?" Ashley grabs the remainder of the deck from him and shuffles while Griffin gathers up the cards on the floor.

"Wow, you're really good at that," Marie-Claire tells her. "You should work in the casino or something."

It took some doing on my part, but Ashley has fit quite nicely into our bizarre little club. I'll confess that things were weird for a while. I felt like a double agent, going back and forth between Katie and Ashley before I finally managed to convince Katie that Ashley wasn't such a bad sort once you got her away from the Jerk Squad. And once Katie and Ashley were square, Marie-Claire and Griffin were fine with her as well. Now Ashley and Marie-Claire are best buddies, and Griffin is in love with her. And it's funny: since Ashley has joined our group, I haven't heard anything more about Marie-Claire's vampire parties. I don't know if Ashley has dragged Marie-Claire out shopping yet, but she's actually started wearing colored clothes. I've never asked Marie-Claire what she was doing in Tim Hortons with a book of crosswords instead of being off partying with college boys like she always told us she was.

I figure that's her secret to share if she ever wants to. After all, it's not like she's covering up a murder or something.

Ashley starts to deal the cards, and she really does look professional doing it. If we were playing something more complicated than Asshole, I might worry that she was some kind of card shark. "So when is Emily moving?" she asks.

"First of the month."

"That's so weird." Katie picks up her cards and starts sorting through them. "That apartment is going to seem so big without her and Wex."

"Well, they're not going far. They're just going to be moving upstairs. I'm sure Wex will be over, like, six times a day. And Dave-the-waiter seems like a nice guy."

"When does Simon start school?"

"At the beginning of June. He's taking some summer classes to update his math and computer stuff, and then he starts full time in September. Accounting. Yawn. But at least he'll be making good money when he's done."

"So weird." Katie grins. "It's nice to hear about good things happening for a change."

"Dude, it's nice to *have* good things happening for a change." I take my worst card, the two of clubs, and hand it to Marie-Claire, who is the janitor this round. She hands me back the ace of hearts.

On the one hand, it's weird that things got back to normal pretty fast after the whole Travis Bingham Incident. On the other, it's not like they went back to the way they were before either. Simon seems more like a human being, for starters. He's starting to talk about his own future as if he's actually got one, and Emily...well, she was getting better even before I told her I'd met Travis. And speaking of Travis, Simon went to see him at work a few days after our breakfast at the Bedrock Bistro. Simon told me they sat in his truck and talked for over an hour, but he wouldn't tell me what they talked about. I guess that's another one of those secrets that's none of my business.

I look around at my odd little group of friends. The funny thing about family, I guess, is that if you don't have the one you need, you can always make your own. People still make fun of Katie for her weight, of Ashley for her spectacular downward social slide, of me for dressing funny (it seems that no one except for my immediate group of friends has noticed I've stopped doing that) and of Griffin for...well, being Griffin. But that's to be expected, I suppose. Anybody who doesn't fit the mold around here gets singled out, even if the mold is broken. And if you've got a safe place to fall, even if it's the International Society of Creeps, Freaks and Weirdos, it's easier to feel like everything will work out all right in the end.

ACKNOWLEDGMENTS

Many thanks to all the friends and early readers who helped out with this project. Thanks especially to my group of Friday Night Crazies—Laura, Joan, Duane, Becky and Linda—and to Lynda Simmons for the notes and encouragement. I wouldn't have gotten to the end without all of you! Also, thanks to my loves, Chuck, Max and Ari, and to my friend Shannon Robinson, who really wanted to find out the ending.

ELIZABETH WENNICK grew up in Germany and Burlington, Ontario, and spent a number of wonderful years on Canada's east coast before moving back to Ontario. Her love of all things artistic has driven her to pursue drawing, knitting, sewing, painting and, most recently, carpentry and furniture design. She has worked at various times as a journalist, arts and crafts instructor, video-store manager, photo-lab technician and personal concierge to ridiculously rich Americans. She has written two novels, a weekly humor column for several southern Ontario newspapers and many short plays, and has co-written two musicals. Elizabeth currently lives in Brantford, Ontario, with her husband, two sons, two cats, a dog and varying degrees of chaos.